THE
MASTER CLASS
COLLECTION

BY RACHEL HAIMOWITZ

RIPTIDE
PUBLISHING

Riptide Publishing
PO Box 6652
Hillsborough, NJ 08844
http://www.riptidepublishing.com

The Master Class Collection

Cover Art and layout by L.C. Chase, http://www.lcchase.com
Editor: Aleksandr Voinov

ISBN: 978-1-937551-01-8

Printed in the United States of America
First edition
March, 2012

Also available in ebook:
ISBN, Master Class: 978-1-937551-01-8
ISBN, Sublime: 978-1-937551-17-9

THE MASTER CLASS COLLECTION

BY RACHEL HAIMOWITZ

RIPTIDE PUBLISHING

TABLE OF CONTENTS

MASTER
CLASS

RACHEL HAIMOWITZ

MASTER CLASS

RACHEL HAIMOWITZ

To my dear friend, business partner, and internet-husband Aleks Voinov, who's been steady and loving at my side since the day we met, helping my dreams come true.

CHAPTER 1

Even stars got star-struck, right? It was perfectly normal. Not embarrassing at all.

At least, that's what Nicky kept telling himself as he stared across the table at Devon fucking Turner, A-lister extraordinaire and, let's face it, hunk to beat all hunks.

And Dom to beat all subs, too. Nicky was certain of it. The way Devon met his eyes with such force across the candle-lit table that Nicky had to avert his gaze. The way he made Nicky feel like the only man in the room, naked at Devon's mercy despite the armor of his three-piece suit and the other six guests at the table, only two of whom he knew but all of whom, he was certain, could see right through his flustered, lust-sick stare.

Shit, he had to get out of here, get some air. Get his head back on his shoulders before it ended up, uninvited, in Devon's lap.

"Excuse me," he blurted, standing up from the table hard enough to skid his chair. He'd forgotten about the napkin in his lap; it swooshed to the floor as all eyes landed on him. Why had he tied his tie so tight? "I uh . . ." He pointed vaguely toward the area where he thought the restrooms were. "Excuse me."

He ran off before he could take stock of all the curious looks. Or, God help him, the knowing one—the absolute, bone-deep surety—of Devon Turner's.

He found the men's room without fuss and pushed through the door, just leaning for a moment on the other side remembering how to breathe. For Christ's sake, this was *ridiculous*. He performed in front of thousands eight times a week without the slightest trouble. What was his problem now?

He cast a glance at the empty urinals and realized he did kind of have to piss. Took care of it with trembling fingers and a visualization exercise or three to keep his Devon-induced erection at bay. Went to the sink to wash his hands and nearly jumped right out of his shoes when the bathroom door opened, and in strode the object of his fantasies.

This time, when Devon's eyes zeroed in on Nicky's, Nicky couldn't look away. Wanted to, didn't want to . . . didn't matter. Somehow, he couldn't move.

Devon stepped forward. Glided, more like—all grace and easy confidence—snatched up one of Nicky's wrists in a powerful hand and pulled him close. No words, which was probably for the best; Nicky doubted he'd have heard them anyway over his heart thudding in his ears or the Vader-esque rasping of his breath. Just a single silent look from Devon, long and piercing, more a statement than a question: *Pay up*, that look said. *Make good on every single thing you haven't been saying for the last hour. I know you. I see you. You see me too.*

Yes. *God* yes.

Nicky didn't struggle when Devon forced his still-dripping hand against his crotch, made him use his pants like a towel—an expensive, pinstriped, tenting towel. Thank God the restaurant was dimly lit; otherwise his erection would show across the room. So would the giant wet spot.

But that was all the thought he gave it as Devon twisted his wrist, forcing Nicky's fingers against his own straining cock. Still Devon watched him carefully, so, so carefully, looking for the argument, the repulsion, the horror. Not expecting to find it, but looking nonetheless. Being responsible.

Nicky ducked his head and thrust his hips forward. *I want what you've got.*

But Devon just yanked Nicky's wrist out to the side and shoved him so hard into the sink that he only stayed (mostly) quiet because Devon slapped one giant paw over his mouth.

He was still breathing through the pain in his back when Devon pulled his hand away and mashed his lips to Nicky's, biting until Nicky opened his mouth in another breathless yell—half surprise, half pain, half *Oh my God I'm being kissed by Devon fucking Turner*, and yes, he was perfectly aware that made three halves, thank you very much. Who could care about things like that anyway when Devon's tongue was parting his lips, when their crotches were grinding together so sweetly that it took only moments before Nicky thought—with what little thought remained—that a water-wet crotch would soon be the least of his problems.

Until Devon stopped, ripping away and shoving Nicky two-handed to the floor.

But that was okay. Heck, *more* than okay. Nicky could play this game. He could play it very, very well.

He swallowed a moan and crawled toward Devon's feet, head down, ass up, inviting—*Take what you want*, his body said. *Beat me, fuck me; preferably both at once.*

"When I'm good and ready, whore." Devon stepped on Nicky's outstretched hand and sneered down at him with positively withering contempt. Nicky's cheeks burned as hot as the tender flesh beneath Devon's heel, but he made no attempt to pull his hand back, to stand up, to take back the offer he'd made. He rather liked it down here, after all. Always had.

But Devon just ran a hand through his hair, straightened his tie, lifted his foot from Nicky's hand, and left the bathroom without another word.

Nicky waited until the door had closed behind Devon before rising to his feet. What the fuck had just happened? If not for the pain in his back and hand, the wetness at his crotch, and the tingle at his lips, he might have doubted it had happened at all. Too good to be true. Too *odd* to be true.

Except for the part where it was.

Bracing his hands against the sink, he blinked into the mirror and tried to compose his face into some semblance of normalcy. He did that for a living, for fuck's sake; why was it so hard now? Faucet. Cold water splashed on hot cheeks with shaking fingers. Towel dry.

His erection was slowly fading. God only knew how long he'd been staring through the mirror, what his friends must be thinking about his absence. He pulled away and forced his feet to carry him back into the dining room—back to his table, to Devon—trying to pretend he wasn't spending every conscious second wondering how Devon's cock would taste shoved down his throat.

CHAPTER 2

"Line?"

From the front row of the empty theater, Nicky's director sighed loudly enough to carry past the mezzanine. The stage manager, clearly bored with feeding Nicky lines, read in a monotone from the script in his lap. "And then he will say to them: Anything you did for one of your brothers here, however humble, you did for me."

Nicky whispered it once to cement it in his brain, then repeated it aloud, eyes roving about his castmates pretending to be sheep on their hands and knees.

He'd not seen too many sheep floating around Manhattan, but he was pretty certain they didn't usually look so pissy.

Of course, he was pretending to be Jesus, and he was pretty certain the son of God didn't grind near-strangers in a men's room and then spend the next day forgetting his lines.

His castmates *baaah'd* in unison. One dead beat followed. Then another. He was really starting to hate this scene.

Robin elbowed him in the shin. *Shit,* his line *again*? He pointed—stage right? No, stage left. "For when I was hungry—"

"*God,* no!"

A-ha-ha, yeah, because that *joke never gets old.*

Nicky threw his director a sheepish (*a-ha-ha*) look and waited for the man to correct him.

"It's 'to the eternal fire, that has been ready for you with the devil and all his angels.' *Then* 'For when I was hungry, blah blah blah. Jesus, Nicky"—and clearly, no joke intended this time—"what's gotten into you today?"

Nicky shrugged. "Sorry, boss. Not feeling very well."

What a lying liar he was. And an idiot, too; here he was in the starring role of fucking *Godspell,* the fucking *Broadway revival* no less, and he couldn't get his head out of his ass. Couldn't stop thinking about dinner last night with his actor buddies and their actor buddies, about what it had been like to sit next to Mr. Devon Turner for an hour and a half.

About what had happened afterward.

"All right, you know what? Go home. Get some rest. Adam, get in there for him."

His understudy peeled out of the house and up onto the stage in two seconds flat, and Nicky, relieved and not nearly as guilty as he knew he should be, offered apologies and a "See you tomorrow" to his castmates. A quick trip to his dressing room to change his clothes and wash the face paint off his right cheek, and then he'd be out of here. The faster he got home, the faster he could jerk off. Or *not* jerk off; he wondered how long he could deny himself tonight before going crazy, if he could manage to sleep without touching himself.

Without thinking of Devon.

He closed and locked his dressing room door, stripped off his Superman t-shirt, and stood in front of the mirror, twisting around with a hiss to examine the soreness at the small of his back. Shame there was no bruise. He pressed two fingers to the tender flesh and hissed again, smiling.

When I'm good and ready, whore, Devon had said. Threatened. *Promised.*

Hopefully he'd be ready soon. Still thinking of dinner (and dessert, definitely dessert), Nicky pulled on a t-shirt and a gray hoodie, jeans and sneakers, hung up his Superman tee, and left the dressing room, the strap of his courier bag slung right across the soreness Devon had caused.

His mind was turned so intently toward yesterday's dinner, toward that moment of instant recognition—his "Domdar" pinging, Devon's "subdar" clearly pinging just as loud—toward Devon's *laissez faire* enjoyment of his food and his drink and all his company *but* Nicky, whom he'd ignored with such finesse after their encounter in the bathroom that Nicky wouldn't even have noticed being ignored if he himself hadn't been staring, fixated, at Devon's hands, Devon's mouth, the casual cruelty just beneath the surface of Devon's boisterous, Ken-doll-handsome face . . .

So inward were his thoughts that when he walked past the last row of seats in the theater, he didn't notice *Devon*.

A hand caught his wrist, squeezing hard, and his first thought was "Oh fuck, crazy fan." Before he could wonder how said fan had gotten into the closed rehearsal, before he could even try to yank his arm away, a big body to match the big hand was pressing into his, lips touching his ear, warm breath whispering, "Not a sound, boy. Not one." A thumb found its way into a pressure point on Nicky's trapped wrist, just daring him to defy the order, but Nicky bit his lip and squeezed his eyes shut, held his breath and nodded.

"Macbeth ruins everything," the whisper continued.

No shit. It was ridiculous to be so superstitious, but at the mention of that cursed play, he couldn't help but cast a glance over his shoulder to make sure there wasn't an electrical fire smoldering in the catwalk or an uncovered trap door on the stage.

"Say it, and it ends the night. 'Macbeth.' Understand?" The thumb dug deeper and Nicky choked off a grunt, nodded again, short and fast. "Say it now. Once. Practice."

"Macbeth," he whispered back, afraid if he spoke any louder, he'd shout, and the whole cast and crew would hear him. They already had enough reasons to be pissed at him.

"Good boy."

Devon yanked Nicky out the auditorium, through the lobby, into the street. Hailing a cab in the Theater District was an art form, but people stopped for Devon Turner. Heck, some people even stopped for Nicky.

A car pulled over in seconds and Devon opened the door, dragged Nicky inside after him. "Manhattan Plaza, please," Devon said to the driver as he fastened his seatbelt, never releasing his punishing hold on Nicky's wrist.

Nicky didn't bother wondering how Devon knew where he lived.

As the taxi merged into traffic, Devon leaned close and brushed his lips against Nicky's ear. "I'm going to fuck you so raw your eyes will water every time you sit." The words were harsh but the tone was a purr, a promise so hot Nicky's breath caught. "Would you like that?"

No breath, no words. Nicky nodded instead.

"I'm going to make you scream. Not my name—just *scream*. Would you like that, too?"

Another breathless nod. He felt Devon's lips curl into a smile against his earlobe, teeth latching on as Devon's thumb, in perfect mirror, bit deep into Nicky's wrist.

By the time they reached his apartment, Nicky was sweating and a little nauseous. The cab ride had been like every Manhattan cab ride, all sudden starts and stops and swerves and the vague stench of the thousands of asses that had warmed the backseat before him.

Devon's grip hadn't let up for a second, and the pain of that pressing thumb was deep, unrelenting, expanding with every passing moment until Nicky could think of nothing else—nothing but Devon, the power of the man, the power Nicky had granted him and just how, exactly, he planned to use it.

Devon didn't let go when they got out of the cab, instead unfastening Nicky's seatbelt for him and dragging him out Devon's door; Nicky had to crawl one-handed across the seat to keep up.

Devon put on a friendly smile for the passersby, the gawkers snapping his photo, the children on the playground between the two towers, the couple in the lobby. He eased up pressure on Nicky's wrist just enough for Nicky to put on a smile of his own.

They made it safely into the elevator without attracting any second glances—at least none of the dubious variety—and when the door closed, Devon shoved him up against the wall hard enough to knock the air from his lungs, pressed tight against him and ground his knee into Nicky's crotch. Nicky's legs unhinged and his cry was swallowed by Devon's mouth ravaging his own, all tongue and teeth and hunger. Still Devon's thumb dug into Nicky's wrist, which had gone so far past painful it was rounding now on numb interspersed with occasional bursts of eye-watering agony.

It was the longest twenty-nine floors of Nicky's life.

He only knew they'd reached his floor because Devon pulled away and dragged him off the elevator. He had no recollection of unlocking his door. Maybe Devon had done it for him. Somehow, they made it to the bedroom, and Devon was tearing Nicky's clothes from him one-handed, yanking and slapping and scratching as he went, letting go of Nicky's wrist only long enough to pull his hoodie and t-shirt over his head.

When Nicky was completely naked and the pincer grip returned to that freshly reperfused pressure point, he cried out and tried to pull away, which made it even worse—so bad, in fact, that for a moment his vision went pure white, and when the room came back he found himself being marched toward the bed, arm wrenched up behind him, cock pointing straight ahead.

"That's right," Devon growled, jerking up on Nicky's wrist, setting off fresh fireworks from his fingertips to his neck. "Scream for me, whore. *Scream*." Another jerk, and Nicky had no choice but to obey.

That strange whiteout again, and this time he came to pressed face-down to his bed, a heavy weight settled across his thighs, another one wedged atop his spine between his shoulder blades, where his wrist was still trapped. He pressed his face into the quilt and bit down hard, roaring into the bedding.

A belt being unbuckled, pants unzipping, the rough scrape of Devon's jeans across his legs. All barely noticed beneath the pain and his own buzzing arousal, the ache of his erection trapped between the mattress and the weight atop him.

A hand drove into the back of his head, slapping hard, then raked down his back. Nicky gasped and arched, gasped again as the movement wrenched his shoulder. Then there were fingers in his open mouth, two, three, a whole hand's worth, scraping against his tongue and his teeth and the back of his throat until he gagged, whimpered, tried to pull away but couldn't move, couldn't buck the weight straddling him or even begin to free his arm, and the first hint of panic set in as Devon laid flat atop him and denied him even the capacity to struggle.

"*Stop*. Hold still!" Devon punctuated his command with another jerk to Nicky's wrist that made his eyes water. That giant hand was still forced into his mouth, so he couldn't scream, not really; the sound built and gathered, though, waiting for the chance to burst free. "No biting, you little fuck!"

This time it was the hand in his mouth that jerked, wrenching his jaw open wide enough for the scream to escape. Then the hand was gone, covered in enough spit, Nicky hoped, to stop him from bleeding when Devon rammed his way inside. He looked over his shoulder as best he could, watching Devon stroke himself with that spit-soaked hand, his cock as large and intimidating as the rest of him, standing out straight and terrifying and beautiful from his unzipped pants.

Devon's eyes were closed, but when he opened them and caught Nicky staring, his hand left his cock and tangled in Nicky's hair. "You like that, whore?" he asked, tugging sharply at Nicky's head.

Speech seemed beyond him just now, but nor could he nod with Devon's fist curled so tight in his hair.

Devon wiggled his hips, cock bobbing against Nicky's ass. "Answer me, or I'll go find another ass to use."

"Yes," Nicky rasped. "Yes, I like it."

"You want it?"

Another teasing wiggle. Even with his head pulled back so far the muscles up the front of his neck hurt, Nicky licked his lips and swallowed, imagining the feel of Devon against the back of his throat, the taste of him as he came. "Yes, please!"

Devon let go of his hair—but not his wrist, still trapped between his shoulder blades and burning like a supernova—and stroked the cheeks of Nicky's ass, delivered one stinging slap, then another. "You're my whore," he growled. His hand left Nicky's ass, and a moment later Nicky heard the sound of a foil packet tearing, the *sqsh sqsh* of a condom being unrolled. "My eager little whore. Say it."

And God, wasn't that the truth, because right now there was nothing in the whole fucking world he wouldn't say or do to feel Devon inside him. Those few words, that small humiliation, was almost too easy.

"I'm your eager little whore, sir," Nicky said, and that was all the encouragement Devon needed.

Devon shoved inside him with ruthless force.

Nicky clenched with the pain, tightening hard around Devon's cock as Devon buried balls deep and began to thrust.

The pounding was as relentless as Devon's grip on his wrist, and in seconds the burn in Nicky's ass was as blinding as the burn in his wrist. Hot shocks of pleasure darted up his belly, his erection roughing over the sheets, the head of Devon's cock roughing over his prostate. The friction was tipping just this side of sweet above the pain, strong enough to taste, to fill his nose and mouth along with the taste of Devon's fingers and the smells of sweat and sex and submission.

Devon was thrusting faster now, his strokes slicker with sweat, the pain still sharp but the burn dulled. Devon leaned forward, pushing into Nicky's wrist and back and ramming his hips so hard the headboard slammed over and over into the wall, so hard Nicky barely heard his cries over the sound of Devon's pleasure, and then Devon shut him up by slamming a hand into the back of his head and shoving his face into the bed, pushing until he couldn't breathe. The fire in his wrist and ass migrated to his lungs, his eyes, his head, set his world floating, spinning, sensations building and building until pleasure and pain were meaningless distinctions, massive knots of *feeling* in the pit of his stomach, the root of his cock, his pounded insides—

Devon yanked his head back just as his world began to fade, leaving him dizzy and high and tingling and gasping for enough breath to scream. Everything hurt beyond reason. His orgasm—ready to burst from him like some alien just seconds before—was far gone now from his grasp. Yet he said nothing, even though he could, nothing but a whimpered "Please . . ." as Devon rammed his ass.

The end came shortly after, awareness of this following only in pieces: cold where warm had been; the pressure gone from his thighs, his back, his arm; emptying relief in his ass; the freedom to curl up on his side, cradling his arm to his chest, staring at the bruises already forming around his wrist. Only as he watched Devon peel off the condom and toss it on the bed by Nicky's chest did he realize he'd cried; a film of tears blurred the scene, but he had no time to wipe them away before Devon stepped forward, grabbed Nicky's hair in one hand and his jaw in the other, and forced his still firm cock down Nicky's throat.

"Lick me clean, whore."

As if Devon even had to ask.

Nicky hollowed his cheeks around Devon's softening cock, laving it with his tongue, chasing down every last drop of cum. He tasted salt, of course, and Devon's musk (a flavor Nicky thought he could come to love, though its bitterness wrinkled his nose now), and the spermicide from the inside of the condom, but none of that, unpleasant as it was, stopped him from doing the best job he could. Nor did the pain still blazing bright through his body, or the look of disgust—so like the one Devon had shot him on the bathroom floor—Devon was leveling at him.

In fact, Nicky realized, shame heating his cheeks, all that only made him love it more.

Devon indicated his satisfaction by shoving Nicky off his cock with a palm between the eyes. He had no clothes to put back on—he'd never undressed in the first place—but he did tuck his dick back into his pants and re-buckle his belt. He paid Nicky not the slightest mind during this process, never so much as cast an eye toward Nicky's jutting erection, which was feeling rather sadly neglected. Nicky inched it toward Devon's hip. Was he not going to return the favor? Jack him off?

Cheeks burning even hotter, Nicky realized he'd probably like it better if Devon left him wanting.

Devon must have realized this, too—after all, who bothered to jack off a whore?—because still he ignored Nicky's straining cock as he dug his wallet out of his pocket and rifled through it. He pulled out a business card, made the briefest of eye contact with Nicky, and tossed it at his face. "Call me," he said. "You have twenty-four hours."

Nicky reached for the card, unable to stop himself from rolling his hips toward Devon, brushing his erection against one clothed leg. The only hint that Devon noticed was a subtle shifting away, out of Nicky's reach, and the rumbling order that followed: "And don't even *think* of touching yourself. I'll know."

Nicky didn't doubt it. He looked forlornly from his throbbing shoulder to his throbbing wrist to his throbbing dick . . . Just one more form of torture, one more way he would let Devon punish him.

Devon was fixing his hair and tie, just like he had at the restaurant. Without the aid of a mirror, he was staring fixedly off into the distance, somewhere over Nicky's head rather than at Nicky.

Before leaving, Devon dipped two fingers back into his wallet, pulled out a twenty, and tossed it on the bed. It landed with a deliberate flutter atop the used condom.

Nicky stared at the money for a moment, mouth hanging open, cheeks and ears burning, anger building in the back of his painfully used throat. Still, he plucked the twenty from the little puddle of semen on the quilt, shook it clean(ish), and carefully folded it into fours before clutching it in one fist for lack of a pocket to stow it in.

By the time he was finished, Devon was gone.

Nicky looked around the room, blinking hard, noticing for the first time that he was in the guest room, not his bedroom. He sat gingerly, wincing as pain flared from ass to head (just as Devon had promised), squeezed his eyes and jaw closed until it passed. The hurt was gradually fading from his shoulder and wrist, and his good hand wandered down to his lap, brushed against his straining cock before he realized what he was doing. He yanked it away and pressed it to his wrist, making himself hiss, then reached for Devon's business card and the phone.

CHAPTER 3

Nicky hadn't expected Devon to answer, so he'd composed a message in his head to leave on Devon's voicemail, half simper and half snark. But at the sound of Devon's voice—his *recorded* voice, for fuck's sake—every muscle in Nicky's body tensed and his tongue took on a life of its own. "Thank you, sir," he found himself saying at the beep. A long moment of silence, of unintentionally heavy breathing into the receiver, passed before he regained control of his mouth and added with a smirk, "Call me back and I'll let you lick my two new dime bags off my ass."

It wasn't a licking his ass was gonna get for saying that. Not a *tongue* licking, anyway. On second thought, maybe saying that hadn't been the best idea, given Devon's . . . prowess.

Nicky slammed down the phone before he could give in to the urge to delete his message. He would *not* be intimidated by this man.

Three Tylenol and one long, hot bath later, he was dead asleep, dreaming of the moment when Devon would finally touch him.

Come morning—well, afternoon, but it passed for morning in Nicky's world—it was no surprise to wake to a sticky mess in his underwear. Another blazing hot shower and three more Tylenol to go with breakfast, along with half the Arts section of the *New York Times*. Only as he was heading out the door did he realize he couldn't recall a single word he'd just read.

The day progressed at an agonizing pace. He couldn't remember the last time rehearsal had dragged this long, felt this drawn out. Or the last time he'd fucked up so much. Even yesterday seemed mild compared to his flubbings today. They had to run "All for the Best" three times because, fuck, who could fucking tap dance and sing at the same fucking time when every motion, every step reignited the brushfires Devon fucking Turner had set?

He left his iPhone in the wings and checked it every time he exited stage left.

Sadly not pursued by a bear, he thought, after three hours and no messages. Not that Devon really was one, unless he'd waxed before that topless scene he'd done in that awful Will Ferrell flick.

There was no point to running lines through dinner, despite his director's not-so-subtle suggestion; he could barely stay focused long enough to do one thing at a time, let alone two. So he fled the theater with a mumbled excuse about needing some air and set off on foot in search of someplace quiet.

Not that there really was such a thing anywhere near the Theater District, but after a further-than-usual walk, he found a close approximation tucked into the corner of 61st and 5th, a little soup and sandwich shop with tiny round tables and floor-to-ceiling windows facing out on Central Park. Devon lived somewhere around here, Nicky realized as he was paying for his panini. He also realized he didn't know what was in the sandwich he'd just ordered. And he never found out, because halfway to the first bite, his iPhone vibrated against his hip.

"Put that sandwich down," Devon said, and Nicky dropped his food and looked wildly out the windows.

"Good boy," Devon drawled, his satisfied smile practically oozing from the speaker holes in Nicky's phone. "Outside, now. Leave it," he added as Nicky went to bus his tray. "Adrienne's, 56th and 8th. Four minutes. Don't be late."

The line went dead.

Four-fifths of a mile in four minutes?

Nicky ran.

Devon was waiting for him outside the restaurant, looking impeccable as always, not a hair out of place. Nicky skidded to a halt a few feet away, panting and self-conscious. The restaurant looked fancy. He was still wearing his Superman tee.

"Here," Devon said as if reading his mind, holding out a navy blue dress shirt and an orange tie that looked like a dead plaid snake.

Nicky took them gingerly and put them on, feeling rather like a tasteless Mets fan (and weren't they all?).

Still, he thanked Devon, because the man had done him a favor— had thought about him carefully enough to realize he'd need one— and that left him feeling strange and squishy in a way that made bad manners impossible.

Devon's eyes followed the progress of Nicky's fingers up the line of buttons on the dress shirt as if contemplating their taste and feel, how satisfying they'd be to suck, to chew—fuck, maybe even to break. It made their task nearly impossible; Nicky fumbled once, twice, a third time with a too-small button hole before Devon nudged Nicky's hands out of the way and did it for him.

"Thank you," Nicky said again. He swallowed the "sir" that tried to follow, felt it hot and heavy on his tongue.

Devon flashed him a strangely admiring smile and said in an equally strange sweet tone, "You clean up really nice."

Nicky smiled back, uncertain. Compliments were acres and miles and whole fucking *continents* away from the things Devon had said to him last night.

Devon shook his head and squashed down a grin with pursed lips, as if he too recognized the disparity. "Come on." He waved toward the restaurant door. "I'm buying you dinner."

It wasn't quite what Nicky had been expecting, but he had a sneaking suspicion he'd enjoy himself anyway. He allowed Devon to usher him inside, one big hand resting on the small of his back.

The restaurant was dim, crowded but quiet, full of expensive décor and expensive suits. He actually recognized a few people—various movie types and members of the Manhattan chattering class.

The waiter handed him the menu without prices. Was it really that obvious who was in charge here?

Well, sort of in charge, he supposed: Devon offered a rueful shrug as he plucked Nicky's menu from his hands.

Nicky smiled curiously, eyebrows raised and head cocked.

"Sorry." Devon squared Nicky's unread menu atop his own, then scratched at the back of his neck. "Mixed signals, I know. But we need to talk. God knows it's the last thing I want to do when I look at you, but I've never been irresponsible with someone before and I don't plan to start now."

Nicky nodded, not sure he agreed—things had gone just fine so far—but of course he'd concede to Devon's desires. "Okay," he said, wishing he still had a menu to play with; he didn't know what to do with his hands and didn't want to fidget in front of Devon.

Devon gave Nicky's fingers a squeeze, firm and self-possessed, called the waiter back, and ordered for them both. So talking, but not as equals. Better that way anyhow. He wouldn't have to say much. If he was lucky, maybe nothing at all.

"Sorry," Devon said, though for what Nicky couldn't figure. Maybe he really was a mind-reader. Or maybe Nicky was just naked in front of him, unable to hide a thing. "When I want something, I . . ." *Take it*, Nicky thought. *Just like you took me.* "Just *looking* at you . . . God. It's hard for me to quiet my instincts for long."

Devon losing control around *Nicky*? That may well have been the most adorable—and ridiculous—thing Nicky had ever heard.

"So help me. Distract me." A wan smile, but not mocking—at least Nicky didn't think so. "Win me over with your wit and charm."

Nicky laughed, then touched his foot to Devon's under the table to make it clear he was laughing with the man rather than at him. Devon made the inevitable Larry Craig joke and Nicky laughed again, realizing only after the moment had passed how completely unselfconscious he'd been. A rare, strange thing, professional liar that he was. It felt good—no, *great*—to be free with this man.

Almost as good as it felt to be bound by him.

They laughed their way through the next hour, and Nicky managed not to think about sex for most of it—until Devon suggested going back to Nicky's apartment to share more wine and conversation.

Actual conversation? Or "conversation" conversation? He didn't know, and he didn't care as long as the one eventually led to the other.

Without another word, he stood from the table and followed Devon into a taxi, calling his stage manager to say he was still under the weather and wouldn't be back tonight. Unsurprisingly, the man made no attempt to talk him out of it.

Devon retained his lighthearted air—a manner Nicky might otherwise have guessed he'd put on strictly for public consumption—in the backseat of the cab. Nicky half expected the man to grab his wrist anyway, even placed it invitingly on Devon's leg. Strange, then, that he couldn't stop himself from flinching when Devon reached for it, that he found himself simultaneously relieved and disappointed when there was no pain. Devon simply held Nicky's wrist in his hand, brushing gently over the bruising with a single finger.

"So lovely," Devon murmured.

Nicky stared at Devon's transfixed expression in the multicolored city lights and thought the exact same thing.

"Does it hurt?"

"You know it does."

Devon stared him in the eye, concerned and maybe just a touch insecure. This was the first time Nicky had ever met a Dom who wasn't too busy pretending he knew everything to notice when he hurt someone for real, and fuck if that wasn't the hottest thing Nicky had ever seen. It made him want to drop to the floorboard and suck down Devon's cock right here in the back of the cab.

No chance for that now, though. Devon might be showing his compassionate side, but he was still, as always, in command. Demanding truth: "Too much?"

Nicky flexed his fingers, turned over his hand and stroked Devon's palm. "You know it isn't. You wouldn't have left me alone last night if it was."

Devon's fingers curled around Nicky's wrist, tightened until Nicky whimpered. At the sound, he smiled a distinctly wicked smile. "I wouldn't have left you alone if I knew you'd blow all your hard-earned money on crack, either."

Just as Nicky was thinking how he'd known that damn message was going to come back to haunt him, Devon's façade crumbled and he burst out laughing, lacing Nicky's fingers in his own and laying their joined hands on his thigh.

It was a very firm thigh.

The moment they got to Nicky's apartment, Devon waved him onto the couch and headed toward the kitchen, as if this were *his* place, as if he had no doubt or question of where anything was. And apparently he didn't, because he returned a minute later with two glasses and a bottle of red. It was less creepy than Devon having known the instant Nicky had sat down to eat at some obscure corner café, but not by much. He couldn't refrain from asking, "How did you—?"

"A magician never reveals his secrets," Devon said with a wink, popping the cork and pouring for them both. An appreciative sniff and then, "My my, Mr. Avery, you do have excellent taste."

The next hour passed in the same pleasant humor dinner had, though being here alone together where the memory of his ravishing was so fresh, Nicky couldn't help but want more than engaging conversation. Devon seemed to share this desire, though he was significantly more disciplined than Nicky was; he'd slid over until their knees touched, had draped fingers over Nicky's bruised wrist but never squeezed. Controlled, teasing. Taking obvious pleasure from watching Nicky squirm and shuffle around the ache of his hour-long erection.

When at last Devon plucked Nicky's glass from his fingers and leaned forward to kiss him, Nicky's eyes fluttered closed and he whispered on a sigh, "Thank you, sir," unaware of his intent to say it until it was out.

He hardly knew what to make of the kiss that followed.

It seemed too sweet, too undemanding. The gentlest pressure, the tang of wine, a curious sweep of tongue across his lower lip, almost tickling. A sigh into his mouth, a caressing hand on his cheek, another wandering up his thigh.

"Mmm," Devon hummed, pulling back just far enough to look Nicky in the eye. When Nicky leaned in for another kiss, the hand on his face curled around his ear and tugged, holding him in place.

"Ah ah ah." Devon swiped a thumb across Nicky's parted lips, poked the tip between them. Nicky took the opportunity to demonstrate what he could do to other, more sensitive parts of Devon's anatomy if given a chance.

Devon closed his eyes, allowing this for a moment before pulling his thumb back and wiping it against Nicky's cheek. "Not yet," he said. "While that mouth clearly deserves an opportunity to worship as many various bits of me and my shoe collection as I can shove in there, we're not done talking yet. To be honest, I never would have guessed that actually letting you speak could be so enjoyable. But hey," a shrug, another gleefully wicked smile, "perfect as I am, even *I'm* wrong sometimes."

A dozen snarky replies flashed through Nicky's head, but he held his tongue. After the strange relaxation of the evening, he was still a little too far out of headspace to handle the kind of abuse that might result from talking back. He'd want it soon, though, now that Devon was finally tightening his grip on the reins.

Devon leaned in for another kiss, slow and sweet and torturous, as if he was planning to nuzzle on the couch all evening rather than start in on the real fun. All well and good—Nicky liked nuzzling well enough. But it wasn't, well, *enough*. If Devon wasn't willing to get things rolling hard in the next few minutes, he'd have to give him a little push.

"Open," Devon said, pulling back again and tapping Nicky on the chin.

Nicky eagerly complied. Would he finally get to taste Devon, to feel that cock filling his throat? The thought of it was so exciting, so consuming, that the taste of wine hitting his tongue almost made him jump.

"Hold still," Devon singsonged, letting the last of the bottle drip onto Nicky's lips. "And don't swallow. Hmm," Devon cocked his eyebrows, clearly amused. "That may be the only time you *ever* hear me say that."

As much as Nicky wanted to obey, Devon had just made him laugh so hard it was either swallow or spew. And somehow, he didn't think Devon would appreciate being sprayed with wine any more than his couch cushions would.

He squeezed his eyes shut as he swallowed both wine and laughter, fully expecting to be punished. When nothing happened, he peeked one eye open to find Devon staring him down, all traces of humor gone.

Nicky flinched as Devon's hand came toward his face, but only a single finger made contact, stroking across the line of his jaw. "Not yet, little one."

A threat, a promise. A trembling, menacing thrill. Nicky shivered beneath the touch.

"You've ruined it. We need more wine. Don't. Move."

Devon grabbed the empty bottle and stalked into the kitchen, but even out of sight, his power, his *force*, lingered like a residue. Nicky was more than ready now for him to unleash it, had already lost his patience for whatever game Devon planned to play with the wine. It was time to take matters into his own hands.

When Devon returned a minute later, Nicky was naked and kneeling on his heels in the middle of the living room. Though Nicky's head was down, he could see Devon stop short in the archway to the kitchen, could *feel* the anger gathering inside him like a static charge.

Nicky grinned.

Until Devon walked right past him to the couch, grabbed the pile of clothes there and threw them at Nicky's head.

"No," Devon said. "Get dressed."

Nicky's eyes snapped up, looking for the meaning behind Devon's words. Had Devon just been fucking with him? Didn't he *want* to punish him?

He reached for his shirt with unsteady hands, pulling it on in silent slow motion—giving Devon a chance to say something, to stop him.

Devon sighed, scrubbed a hand down his face. The change in his demeanor was so sudden it seemed as if he'd physically wiped away Dom-Devon to reveal some strange sweet other-Devon hiding beneath. Or maybe that was just part of the control, part of the mind-fuck; surely Devon could no sooner shed the need to dominate than Nicky could shed the need to submit.

"Come on," Devon said, patient and encouraging, like a father walking his child to the first day of school. "This . . ." One big hand, pointer finger out, gestured rapidly back and forth between them. "This isn't going to work. You can't have it both ways. I need more than that from you. You want to play? Fine. Good. Great, even; I want to play, too. God knows, you're—" his eyes widened, took in Nicky's half-dressed form with naked appreciation, "funny and smart and talented and, you know, not *too* hard to look at. But it's pretty obvious nobody's ever bothered to train you, and I don't take in strays. So get dressed, sit down, come back to Earth, and let's talk contract."

CHAPTER 4

D evon plunked down on his couch with his digital recorder and closed his eyes, steadying and centering himself, letting the part of him that was powerful, demanding, king of its domain come fully to the fore. Both the dungeon and the living room were set up, his favorite toys laid out, the evening carefully mapped in his head.

He reviewed last night's negotiations over and over, listening to the digital recording, to the nuances in Nicky's voice as he'd answered Devon's questions. Not that there was much to review; Nicky had said very little, refused to cop to favorite toys or techniques. He'd just insisted over and over, "No limits. You can't pull me out of a scene with pain."

Devon even believed that, given the extremity of their first encounter and the state in which he'd left Nicky—desperate, blueballed, unable to wait so much as ten minutes before calling him to beg for more.

Of course, he'd also cracked wise about the $20 Devon had left, which was why it came as no surprise when Nicky said he'd always push Devon—*always*, despite Devon's insistence that always was a damn long time.

By the end of their talk, the only concrete ground he'd gotten from Nicky was "No marks that will show on stage" and "You can come in my mouth all you want—in fact, please do—but don't spit in it. Grosses me out." Devon could abide those both, though the latter made him chuckle and the former he truly regretted.

He wished there'd been more, though, something solid to use as a guide. He liked Nicky, liked him a lot, which was why he felt so uncomfortable with so little having been said. He'd sensed the depth of Nicky's need, and even more troubling, a clear lack of self-insight. If Nicky had any idea why he wanted—no, *needed*—what he found in Devon, he hadn't given the slightest hinting of it. Strange how someone could seem so inexperienced in some ways, yet clearly so confident and well-versed in others.

Then again, Nicky did pretend to be things he wasn't for a living. Heck, they both did. And maybe that was the real problem.

But he couldn't deny the affection or desire he felt for Nicky—for the *real* Nicky, the one he'd caught a glimpse of in a restaurant last week and again last night. So different from the young man he'd watched mature across five seasons of *Prey*; from the sexy-slinky drag queen he'd coveted from the orchestra in last year's run of *Priscilla, Queen of the Desert*; from the patient, paternal savior he'd seen in the *Godspell* rehearsal where he'd claimed Nicky. Devon wanted very much to delight the man, to show him how much pleasure he could find in his *own* skin, to make this good and right for them both.

But first, Nicky would have to earn it.

Nicky came over straight from rehearsal, dressed for the occasion in a suit and tie (and sneakers, the little brat) as Devon had ordered, already well on his way into subspace. His eyes were downcast. He said not a word, even in greeting, and he made no move to come inside until Devon said, as if talking to an idiot, "Don't just stand there. People will stare."

A smile flashed across Nicky's face like maybe that idea appealed to him, but then it was gone and he was standing in the foyer, head down, quiet and pliant as a doll. Waiting.

Testing Devon.

"Shoeless house," Devon said, turning his back on Nicky and making himself comfortable on the couch. "Leave them by the door."

Nicky obeyed, and when he was done, Devon added, "Take off your coat and hang it up." He pointed toward the hall closet. "Suit jacket, too. And your tie."

Again, Nicky obeyed in silence. No hesitation, no delay. But Devon did hear something swish to the floor as Nicky finished and stepped away.

"Did your coat fall?"

"No, sir."

"Your suit jacket, then?"

This time, though Nicky's gaze was still on the floor, half his mouth crooked up into a smile. "No, sir."

Devon sighed; he could already see how this was going to go. He'd expected this behavior though, and if Mr. Topping from the Bottom thought he could get a rise out of him that easy, he had something else coming.

Calmly, but with inarguable firmness, Devon stood. "Tell me what you dropped."

"What looked like a very expensive topcoat. Sir." Nicky ducked his head, but not before Devon saw that mischievous smile grow.

"That's one for carelessness and another for attitude," Devon said, maintaining his soft calm, his neutral expression. "Pick it up."

His fingers twitched at his sides, itching to hit, when Nicky chirped, "Whatever pleases you, sir."

God, that little . . . "That's three now, boy."

Well, at least he was doing as he was told.

When Nicky was done hanging the coat (and thankfully didn't "drop" anything else), Devon ordered him to heel. Nicky walked to the center of the living room, between the couch and the coffee table, looking effortlessly breathtaking in his fitted shirt and suit pants. Devon was getting hard just looking, never mind actually *touching,* but no . . . it would be an hour yet, at least, before either of them would be getting off. And damn it, but the man was looking awfully damn smug.

Devon crossed his arms and glared. "I'm sure that cutesy little brat act works elsewhere, but here, we play *my* games, not yours. Give me your left hand."

Devon held out his right hand, and Nicky placed his left in it, palm to palm. "This game is called 'You Answer My Questions Truthfully and I Won't Have to Punish You.' Not a very creative title, I know, but it's not as if I have someone to impress, now is it." As Devon spoke, he pulled the cufflink from Nicky's French cuff, watching Nicky watch him with a sparkle of excitement in those bright blue eyes.

Nicky's hand was a little cold but his pulse was racing. He clearly thought he was being undressed, was clearly excited by that (the evidence not just in his eyes), and was clearly, sadly mistaken.

"Double-sided backs?" Devon turned the silver cufflink over in his left hand, his right hand still gripping Nicky's wrist. "My, Nicky, I didn't think you the type to splurge for this kind of class."

"There's a lot you don't know about me. Sir."

Devon didn't like the way Nicky kept tacking on "sir" as an afterthought, but it didn't surprise him—more testing, more tug-of-war. He gave Nicky's bruised wrist a hard squeeze to make his displeasure clear, despite knowing that was exactly what Nicky wanted. "That's four, smartass." Four of what he had no idea yet, but he'd figure it out soon enough. "You're a man of many secrets, huh?"

Nicky's smile faded and he shrugged, unreadable eyes settling on Devon's face for one second before Devon smacked him across the side of the head hard enough to send him to the floor. Nicky cried out, landed on his knees and his one free hand. He looked suitably shocked: Devon's precise intention.

Nicky made no attempt to rise, or to free the wrist Devon was still holding. He simply rubbed with his left hand at the spot Devon had hit. If the tightness in his jaw was any indication, it was hurting quite a bit. Or maybe he was just pissed. Probably both.

Devon wondered if he'd blown the deal—bedroom violence rarely bore any resemblance to real violence, and many he'd been with in the past couldn't tolerate the blurring of the two—but outwardly he offered only an arch, "Don't worry, I aimed for the head, not the face. No marks, pretty." He yanked Nicky to his feet, growling, "And don't look so surprised. You had that coming and you damn well know it. Now answer my question."

Nicky opened his mouth but then closed it. Opened it again, brows furrowed. When Devon's free hand twitched in the silence, Nicky flinched. *Good.*

"I'm sorry, sir, I forgot the question."

Was that another attempt to goad him? Nicky seemed more sincere than he had before, but surely Devon hadn't cowed the boy with just one strike—not after all the abuse he'd dished out in their first encounter. Still, Devon decided to treat it as if he had. If Nicky was playing him, then he wouldn't get the punishment he was seeking, and if he was being truthful, then he would see that Devon was willing to reward honest requests for help.

Devon gave Nicky's wrist a gentle squeeze. "That's okay, Nicky. Never be afraid to ask me for help."

Nicky nodded once, faintly, his expression strange and once again unreadable. Still holding his wrist, Devon circled around behind him, pressing Nicky's hand into the small of his back. Nicky kept it there even when Devon let go.

"I said, 'You're a man of many secrets, huh?'"

"I like to keep my own counsel, sir." Nicky's eyes tracked Devon as he completed his circle, stopped in front of Nicky, and grabbed his other wrist, removing that cufflink, too.

"There will be no secrets here. You belong to me. Your thoughts, your feelings, your fears. They're not yours to keep. Do you understand?"

There was that startled look again, like Nicky hadn't heard this before. Like he didn't know what to make of it. Maybe his previous play had all been shallow, his other Doms nothing more than pretty faces with cuffs and whips: weak wills Nicky could fool, master actor that he was.

If that were true, then Nicky had never truly let go before. Never trusted enough to turn himself over completely. The thought felt lonely and unclean, like a used condom lying in a gutter. It saddened Devon, redoubled his determination to show Nicky that play could be so much more than an empty transaction.

"That's five for making me wait," he said when the pause had stretched too long. "I said, do you understand?"

"Yes, sir," Nicky mumbled, dropping his gaze to the floor.

Devon lifted Nicky's chin with one finger and locked eyes with him. "No, you don't. But you will. You will. First step? Obedience training."

Devon stepped behind him again, drawing Nicky's other arm around to cross the boy's wrists at the small of his back. He gathered up the material of both shirt cuffs and pushed the shaft of one cufflink through all four holes, pinning them together. "Can you feel what I'm doing here?"

Nicky shook his head. "No, sir."

"You had one expensive cufflink too many. Tug, but gently. Don't undo my work."

Nicky carefully uncrossed his wrists about an inch before the material caught, halting him. He felt around with his fingers, slender curious digits groping at the cloth until they stumbled across the single binding cufflink.

Still safely out of Nicky's sight, Devon allowed himself to close his eyes for just a moment, imagining those fingers groping at him. He had no doubt of their prowess, their skill, if allowed the freedom to roam.

When he opened his eyes again, he had to tear them from Nicky's hands.

"Get it?" he asked, coming around to face Nicky. He was glad Nicky had lowered his head like a good little sub, glad he didn't have to be tempted into rashness by such a lovely face, by the urge to shove his cock down that throat until Nicky choked.

"Yes, sir."

"I won't bother to threaten you with what will happen if you break it. You *will* hold yourself still."

"Yes, sir."

"Good boy."

Devon settled on the couch, out of Nicky's line of sight but still within arm's reach, leaned back, and crossed his legs—a pleasant pressure on the hard-on he'd been sporting since Nicky had removed his jacket. He picked up the riding crop he'd placed earlier on the cushion beside him and rolled it between his fingers, studying the man in profile. Though Nicky hadn't moved his head, Devon knew he was watching the toy from his peripheral vision.

"Tell me why you're here, Nicky."

"Because you told me to come."

Devon leaned forward and thwacked Nicky once, sharp, on his bound hands. Nicky's fingers curled and he hooked the middle ones together, ostensibly to stop himself from breaking apart the tenuous cufflink bond.

But Devon knew better—those middle fingers were sticking out a little too much, telling Devon where he could shove it.

"That's six, smartass. Try again. Why are you here?"

Nicky bit his lip and rocked a little before conceding, "For sex."

That pulled a chuckle out of Devon. "So you're a slut, huh?"

"Yes, sir."

"A whore? Selling your obedience for a hard fuck?"

"And $20, last I checked. Sir."

It took every ounce of control Devon had not to burst out laughing. He didn't strike Nicky, either, since that was so clearly what the boy wanted. Instead, he pretended he simply hadn't heard the quip. "I don't believe you. This isn't about sex."

More rocking, the movement subtle but nervous to Devon's eyes. "No, sir?"

Devon cropped Nicky's hands again. "That's seven. Don't speak out of turn."

Silence. Devon waited for an apology that never came. Good— the boy was better trained than he'd let on.

"Now tell me why you're here."

Nicky sighed, flexed his fingers and rolled his shoulders. Nervous? Uncomfortable? Confused? Exasperated? Devon couldn't quite tell it was all of the above until Nicky mumbled, "To lose control."

"What?" Devon asked, raising his voice and cupping a hand to his ear. "Speak up!"

"To lose control!" Nicky said, mimicking Devon's tone exactly. "Sir!"

Nicky's honesty, however snarky, earned him a strike on the back of the neck, much more than a swat and painful enough to make his shoulders hunch. He hissed through a smile that faded when Devon drawled, "You've never lost control a day in your life. But," he added, thoughtful, "I think you really want to. Do you want to?"

"If it pleases you, sir."

Of *course* he'd say that. The perfect answer in that perfectly neutral, perfectly subservient tone. And yet he'd managed to turn it into a stick with which to poke the sleeping bear, rather than an offering to pacify. What he didn't realize yet, though, was that Devon could put up with an awful lot of poking. He'd bite when he damn well felt like it and not a second before.

Devon smiled with deliberately measured patience. "Tell me why, Nicky."

Even from the side, Devon could see Nicky's eyebrows rise. "Why, sir?"

Devon cropped his hands again, a teasing blow. But Nicky's fingers must have been getting sore, or maybe just tired—he laced them all together this time.

"That's eight. Don't play stupid with me. I know better. Why do you want to lose control?"

Another sigh, like answering these questions was work, a cruelty, more unpleasant than the punishments you actually didn't enjoy. He rocked on his feet, fidgeted with the edge of one French cuff, and finally said, "I, I don't know, sir."

Devon let the silence stretch, unwilling to give Nicky the blow he wanted. Unwilling to speak for him, to let him off the hook.

Nicky rocked some more, bouncing on his toes, almost taking a step. Testing Devon again? Well, Nicky's arms would get tired long before Devon would ever get bored with staring at him.

"I, uh, I like to let go. Not have to think." Nicky shrugged apologetically, as if he knew what he was saying was clichéd, expected, the sort of answer you gave because it was the one your Dom wanted. Yet Devon got the impression of sincerity, and he was rarely wrong about such things. "At work, you know, whole shows succeed or fail because of me. Ever since *Prey*"—the little indie cable show that could—and did—for five years, the one that made Nicky's career— "everywhere I go, someone wants a piece of me. I get . . . tired. Theater used to relax me, you know? No crazy shooting schedules, I got to sing, dance, goof around. But eight shows a week on Broadway? God, that's pressure."

Devon rewarded Nicky's introspection with another hard strike to the neck, this time just below his left ear. Nicky's eyes closed a moment, not tight like Devon had expected, but softly, in ecstasy. A tiny release. Poor guy was wound so tight.

Devon leaned back and recrossed his legs. "Oh. I see. Poor little famous actor. So much *responsibility*." Jazz hands here, with the crop still in one, wiggling by Nicky's hip. "I'm a famous actor too, you know. Don't see me asking someone to treat me like a six-year-old. But that's what you want, isn't it."

Ah, that look of shocked surprise again. Devon was coming to treasure that look.

"N-no sir, I—"

"Oh really? You've had your every whim catered to your whole life. I bet you've never been punished for anything, have you? That's why you're here. To be punished. To be put in your place. To be made small."

The surprise on Nicky's face traded place with annoyance. "I haven't had 'my every whim—'"

"Bullshit. Look at you. Glam-actress mommy, big producer daddy. Plenty of money. Fucking Dustin Hoffman over for Sunday brunch. Talent to spare, looks to die for. Never even had to *audition* for work with connections like that; shit just fell in that pretty little lap of yours while your castmates were living eight to an apartment and subsisting on Ramen noodles. Then comes your big hit show, your own fame, your own money, your own fucking dressing room on 45th Street. People throwing themselves at your feet your whole life. Oh, and that's nine, by the way."

Nicky's fidgeting had stopped. He was trembling now, his hands clenching into fists behind his back. He was angry. Furious. In way over his head.

But exactly, Devon believed, where he really, secretly, deep down wanted to be.

Devon got up, stood right in Nicky's face and whispered, calm as ever, "You don't even know what it *means* to lose control. You've never lost anything in your life."

"That's not—!"

Devon cut him off with a rough hand over his mouth, the other pressing to the back of his head to keep him from pulling away. "Ten. And you *hate* it. You *hate* being so blessed. You feel *guilty*. You think you don't *deserve* it. So you skip around from one so-called 'Dom' to the next, punishing yourself, bringing yourself down, seeing how the other half lives where things are hard, where things *hurt*, where someone's always trying to tell you what to do." Nicky roared into Devon's hand and Devon wrenched Nicky's head, silencing him. "Except it never works because you fucking *cheat*. You drop coats and you talk back and I bet you miscount when they flog you, and they do what *you* want them to do and never even notice they're being played! Well guess what, Nicky." Devon leaned in until his lips brushed the shell of Nicky's ear. "I'm smarter than that. And that shit won't fly here."

He shoved Nicky away with both hands, toward the coffee table. Nicky stumbled over it and fell hard on his ass. Somehow, the cufflink didn't pop, so he dragged himself to his knees and then his feet without using his hands, chest heaving, nostrils flared, jaw locked so hard Devon thought his teeth might crack. But Nicky wanted this, surely he must, because he stepped back to his spot by the couch and turned his eyes back to the floor, burning a hole through Devon's carpet with the heat of his glare.

Devon stood before him and whispered, low and dangerous, "Say it, Nicky. Tell me you're spoiled. Tell me you've never tasted denial. Tell me you hate it."

Silence stretched between them, Nicky still burning holes in the floor, still breathing hard. Devon was proud he'd pushed him into honest emotion, honest reaction, but he was also starting to wonder what the fuck he was supposed to do *now*, how he could keep moving him forward, when Nicky saved him by gritting out, "No."

"Oh really?" Devon drawled. A raised eyebrow, crossed arms. Deliberate nonchalance—*you can't faze me, boy.* "And why not?"

Still fuming, forcing every word through clenched teeth, "Because it's not true."

Nicky waited, oozing resentment, for permission to continue.

It never came. Devon simply stared for a moment, then turned on his heel and left the room.

"Wait!" Nicky called as Devon reached the hallway. "Aren't you going to punish me?"

Devon flashed a wolfish grin over his shoulder. "Yes. How many do you have coming again?" He knew the answer, just wanted to see if Nicky had been paying attention—and if he had, whether or not he'd test Devon by inflating it.

But Nicky said simply, "Ten, sir."

"Right. Three minutes time-out apiece. That's half an hour. Don't. You. Dare. Fucking. Move. Not an inch, is that clear?"

Without waiting for an answer—without even a glace back at the shock and irritation no doubt marring Nicky's perfect face—Devon strode into his bedroom and slammed the door.

CHAPTER 5

Devon flopped back on his bed and scrubbed his hands across his face. He was almost glad Nicky had refused to speak—he was worn bordering on exhausted, tense and vibrating and unbearably horny. Nicky was . . . a *challenge*. He hadn't had this much fun in years.

He wondered what Nicky was doing right now, if he was still standing stunned and fuming in the middle of Devon's living room, hands cufflinked behind his back. Probably, at least for the moment.

God, just the *thought* of it made his balls ache.

Devon unzipped his jeans and freed his erection, giving in to his own need for the first time in what felt like hours, like days, like a marathon of focused denial. He closed his eyes and pictured Nicky's fingers dancing over those French cuffs; the perfect, astonished parting of Nicky's lips when Devon had struck him; the grim set of that sculpted jaw clenched against pain and unpleasant truths.

Then that jaw opened wide as he fucked Nicky's throat, those lips stretched wet and pliant around him, those fingers unbound just long enough to fondle his balls or maybe, if he were a very lucky slave, to penetrate him as he sucked him off. Devon's fist around his erection became Nicky's—loving, worshipful, masterfully skilled—and he came in seconds, biting his lips lest he make a sound Nicky might hear.

When his heart and his breathing had settled, he lay for a moment with his eyes closed, listening carefully for sounds from down the hall. Nothing so far, though he hadn't expected Nicky to misbehave quite so quickly. But he knew the boy would eventually; it hadn't taken Devon ten minutes to figure out that being alone was the worst kind of torture for Nicky. He purposefully hadn't even left Nicky a distraction—hadn't bound him tight enough to struggle against, hadn't blindfolded or gagged him, hadn't shoved a plug up his ass, nothing.

Devon stood and stripped, still thinking of Nicky as he stepped into the shower. Poor thing was probably bored silly, confused, angry, maybe a little hurt. Wondering how he'd lost control and if he really wanted this, after all. Touching Devon's stuff, maybe? Looking at his CD collection? Watching TV? Being naughty, Devon was certain, in the hope he'd misunderstood Devon's words, that Devon would come back out there and beat him until he came and then kick him out until next time.

Or would he just say "fuck it" and leave?

Hmm. Better not keep him waiting *too* long. Thirty minutes was an agony of forever when you were just standing there counting the seconds—and perhaps the one agony Nicky couldn't endure without help.

Devon soaped up and rinsed off, elected not to shave (the image of rubbing his stubbled cheek along Nicky's bare stomach nearly had him jacking off again), put on clean jeans and a long-sleeved polo (Nicky hadn't yet earned the right to see any skin), and snuck back into the living room just twenty-three minutes after he'd left.

Sure enough, Nicky was putting down a picture on the mantel and rushing back to his spot in the middle of the room. And his hands were free, though he was holding them behind his back now, trying to arrange himself as if he hadn't moved. At least he had the decency to look guilty.

Devon stopped dead in the archway, pointed at the front door, and snapped, "Go home."

Nicky's eyes flicked from the floor to Devon and back again, and in that second, Devon saw everything he'd hoped for: shock, hurt, bewilderment.

And just as Devon had expected, Nicky neither spoke nor moved.

Devon held his ground, kept the hardness in his tone and on his face. "I mean it, Nicky. I'm not playing. This apartment's only big enough for one Dom, and until you get that, I'm done with you. Go home."

Nicky looked right at him, mouth hanging open. Devon cut him off before he could even begin to argue, one accusing finger pointed square at Nicky's chest, voice raised to match. "You don't deserve me. Why should I waste my time on some bratty little whore who only wants someone to beat him until he can get off without guilt, huh? Someone who can't follow a simple fucking direction. You don't even want what I'm offering! You don't want to find yourself; you want to get lost." Devon stalked to the closet, grabbed Nicky's coat, and hurled it at him. "So get lost."

Nicky stood there dumbly, holding the coat in both hands like he had no idea what it was or how it worked. He looked sick, pale, on the fence between tears and fury. But he came down exactly where Devon had thought he would: on his hands and knees at Devon's feet.

"Please, sir." Nicky pressed his forehead to the floor just centimeters from Devon's bare toes. "I . . . I don't want to go."

Devon nudged him on the cheek with his foot. "Bullshit."

Nicky inched forward and placed a kiss on the top of Devon's foot. Devon responded with a little kick. Though it clearly hurt and probably frightened Nicky—bruises there would be hard to explain or cover—the boy kept his hands out of the way, leaving himself exposed. "Please, sir, I do! I do want what you have to give! And I don't . . . I know I don't deserve it but if you'd please just give me another chance, I'd do anything, sir. I'll stand here like a statue the whole night. Just please let me show you I can be behave, I can be worth your time!"

Another kiss to Devon's big toe, a moment of wet heat that ran straight to his cock. He held still, and Nicky took that as permission to kiss again, bolder and wetter, panting and frantic to prove himself.

Devon allowed this for a bit before pulling his foot away and stepping on Nicky's head. "All right, Nicky, one more time. Why are you here?"

"Because . . . because you're right," Nicky whispered, half muffled by the carpet, half muffled by his own reticence. "I do hate how easy it all is."

Devon stepped back and said almost kindly, "Get up. Hang up that coat. And this time, *don't* drop anything."

CHAPTER 6

Devon spent almost thirty minutes tying Nicky up. He worked with silent, focused efficiency, choosing rope over leather or steel, wanting the intimacy and intricacy of rigging over the fast and generic cuffs and chains hanging along one wall of the dungeon. He wanted to show Nicky he was worth the time and effort, that these encounters could be so much more than a mechanical beating and a rough fuck.

Devon looped coil after coil of cord around slim wrists and ankles, sculpted biceps and thighs, formed interlocking diamonds across naked shoulders and chest and back. Nicky's was a dancer's body, all lean lines and honed power. Devon worked it with an artist's hands, a model-maker's eyes, his finished product a frieze of stunning beauty. Someday, he thought with a burst of fierce and admittedly premature possessive pride, he would show off that beauty to a select, lucky few.

For all its aesthetic pleasure, Devon's rigging was hardly restrictive. Nicky was still firmly on the floor, could bring his legs together or apart as he wished, could move his hands and arms a foot in any direction. His legs were spread only because Devon had positioned him that way—the tethers linking his wrists and ankles to the large steel frame Nicky was standing within were too long to serve any real purpose. Only the rope leading from Nicky's chest to the top of the frame would restrict him; it would keep him from falling if his legs gave out.

Devon planned to make damn well sure they would by evening's end.

But for now, Nicky had lessons to learn, and control was at the top of the list.

Devon finished tying his last knot and said, "Close your eyes."

Nicky smiled and gave the ropes around his wrists a tug. "What, no blindfold, sir?" But he did as he was told, so he didn't see the slap that landed across his cheek a second later.

"You beg me to let you show me how good you can be and the first thing you do is speak out of turn? That's one, by the way."

The smile fell from Nicky's face and he opened his mouth as if to apologize, then thought the better of it and dropped his chin.

"And no, no blindfold. A blindfold is a privilege. It has to be earned. When you prove to me you can keep your eyes closed on your own, then maybe I'll permit you the luxury of a blindfold. And when you prove to me you can hold still on your own . . ." Devon grabbed the rigging at Nicky's chest and pulled him forward until he tilted off his feet. The ropes took his weight, instantly turning his pale skin a satisfying shade of pink. "Then maybe I'll permit you the luxury of a nice, tight rigging." A hard shove knocked Nicky back onto his feet, and he rearranged himself how Devon had last put him without being told.

"And if, and this is a *big if,* you can prove to me you're capable of communicating well when asked and keeping quiet when not, then maybe, just *maybe*, I will permit you the luxury of being gagged by my cock before I send you home."

Was that a little whimper? Nicky licked his lips, sighed softly and wrapped both hands around his tethers. His eyes remained securely closed, his brow furrowed a little as if he were afraid he might slip up and open them by accident.

"But that's for later. For now, I'm going to do things to you, and you will tell me exactly what those things are. Understand? Speak."

"Yes, sir." Nicky's brow furrowed a little deeper. Parsing, Devon thought, working through what the point of this was, how it would go, if he would like it.

Devon placed his fingertips on either side of Nicky's chest and ran one thumb lightly over a nipple. Nicky jumped, gasped softly, and—just as Devon had expected—completely forgot to talk.

"That's two. Speak, Nicky. What am I doing?" Another swipe of thumb over nipple, another intake of breath. And a raging hard-on.

"You're, you're touching my nipple."

Devon stilled his hands. "Not good enough. More."

That crease between Nicky's brows grew deeper still, and a frown formed on his lips to match. "Um, your hands, no, fingertips. Your fingertips are touching my chest. And um, your—" Devon swiped across both nipples this time, and Nicky's breath hitched again. "Your thumbs? Your thumbs are rubbing across my nipples."

"Good," Devon said, rewarding Nicky with a hard pinch to the peaked flesh. Nicky's head dropped back and his mouth fell open.

"No. Focus."

Nicky lifted his head and Devon took the boy's wrists in his hands, moved Nicky's arms straight out to his sides, parallel to the floor.

"You're lifting my arms."

"Yes, good. Keep them that way." Next his feet; he nudged the insides of Nicky's ankles with his crop until Nicky spread his legs far enough past shoulder width to put a strain on him.

"That's a . . ." Again, his closed eyes squeezed tighter, and his teeth dragged over his lower lip. Poor thing, this was harder for him than a caning. "A crop? You're tapping my ankles. The insides. Making me spread my legs."

"Good." Devon delivered three hard slaps with the crop to the inside of Nicky's right thigh.

Nicky hissed through his teeth and his toes curled, but this time he kept his head up. "You, uh." A hard swallow, that lithe tongue darting out to moisten his lips again. "You hit me with the crop."

"More." Devon rubbed the crop over the area he'd just struck, a bright shade of pink amidst the sparse auburn hairs.

"On the thigh. Inside, right. Halfway between my knee and my crotch. Now you're rubbing the spot."

Two more slaps, a pause, three more. Hard, focused. On the sixth strike to that same two-inch patch of skin, Nicky's foot came off the ground, his knee tucking in to protect his thigh.

"*Down!*" Devon roared, his voice filling the room before dying against the soundproof walls. Nicky flinched and put his foot back on the floor. His fingers wrapped around his wrist tethers, squeezing tightly.

"You, uh," Nicky cleared his throat, and Devon detected a hint of a rather naughty smile. "You yelled at me."

Devon smacked the crop against Nicky's bobbing cock and laughed. "Smartass."

He exchanged the crop for a Wartenburg pinwheel and ran it up the inside of Nicky's extended arm, wrist to shoulder, applying light pressure.

Nicky shivered, goose bumps rising in the wake of the wheel. "That's, uh . . ." Another little frown, brows furrowing deep. "One of those little spiky metal wheels, right?"

"Very good." Devon ran it back from shoulder to wrist, pushing harder.

Nicky's breathing sped up. "You're running it down my arm."

"How does it feel?"

"Feel, sir?"

Devon chuckled, but it felt a little forced. "Yes, Nicky, *feel*. You know, that thing normal people do every day as they go through life, interacting with others and their environment."

"Um, good?"

Devon froze the wheel. "That's three. Try again."

Devon looked on at the now-predicable brow furrow, the slightly parted lips. "Sharp. Prickly. Hurts a little. It's cold." Nicky flexed his fingers around the rope—his arms must be getting tired—and added, "Gives me the willies. But in a good way."

Devon resumed his rolling, back up the arm, pushing much harder.

"Rolling the wheel again, up my arm, across my chest." Nicky's voice was getting tight, thick. A sharp gasp as the pinwheel went over one nipple, then the other—Devon could see him fighting to stay still—and Nicky added, "Hurts a lot now."

Devon backed up the pinwheel and rolled it over a nipple again. "And how does that make you feel?"

"I . . ." Devon stopped the wheel with a tine poking deep into one nipple, rocking it minutely back and forth. Nicky was beginning to vibrate, to struggle with his lack of restraints. "I like it."

Devon let up the pressure but didn't remove the wheel, promising more if Nicky was good. "That's nice, but that's not what I asked. How does it make you *feel*?"

Nicky stepped back a few inches and tossed his arms in sudden— and expected—exasperation. "Fuck, Devon!" he growled, his eyes popping open and narrowing immediately into a glare. "Are you gonna fuck me or sit me on your couch and ask me about my mother!"

Devon crossed his arms and arched an eyebrow toward Nicky's hands, which were now curled into fists and hanging by their tethers a few inches from his thighs.

"I thought we might do both." He shrugged. "Minus the couch of course. Bad boys don't get to sit on the comfortable furniture." His smirk fell away and he reached for Nicky's throat, grabbing hard. Nicky's grunt of surprise—*or is it panic?*—vibrated against his palm. "Now you listen to me, boy. Only two things are allowed to come out of that pretty little mouth of yours, and my name isn't one of them." A shake, a squeeze that made Nicky's eyes water. "Do you understand me?"

Nicky had no air to speak, so he nodded instead. He coughed when Devon let him go, slumped for a moment against the rigging. His hands tried to rub at his neck but the tethers stopped them several inches short.

Devon gave him a few seconds to recover before slapping him lightly, right cheek and then left. "Prove it."

"Sir?" Nicky asked, carefully repositioning himself how he'd been before—Da Vinci's Vitruvian Man. His arms were trembling; his shoulders were surely achingly tired by now.

"What two things can you do with that mouth besides hope and dream you might one day earn the honor of pleasuring me with it?"

"Um." Nicky swallowed, grimaced. Devon could see the impressions of his fingers low on Nicky's neck, where his tie would go when he dressed to leave. Good—it would remind Nicky of him every time he turned his head. "I can, uh, answer your questions?"

"Yes. And?"

The poor thing looked desperately confused, but Devon could see the instant when realization hit; Nicky slumped, deflated, and mumbled, "Or safeword."

Again, Devon reached for Nicky's neck, but this time he wrapped his fingers behind it and drew Nicky forward, biting the boy's lip and thrusting his tongue into his mouth. Nicky whimpered beneath him, half startled pain, half pleasure, and Devon shoved him away. "Well what do you know. You're not as stupid as you seem after all. I believe that calls for a reward—though don't think I've forgotten to count; you're up to four now. Eyes closed, Nicky, the rules haven't changed."

Once Nicky closed his eyes, Devon fished some lengths of rawhide and a set of small iron weights from a drawer. He wound one strip tightly around Nicky's scrotum, seating the testicles as far down as they'd go and tightening the skin around them before binding them in place. Nicky grew hard again at the handling. He was also beginning to sweat a little, the muscles in his widely spread legs and arms overtaxed and trembling.

"You like CBT?" Devon asked as he finished binding off Nicky's nuts.

"Yes, sir."

Devon made a loop at the bottom of the rawhide tie and hooked on the first weight, letting it dangle between Nicky's knees. Nicky's eyes shut a little tighter. "You're a regular little pain slut, aren't you."

"Yes, sir," Nicky said with a distinct hint of pride. And also a hint of challenge.

"Legs tired?"

"Very, sir."

Devon retrieved his crop. He wasn't usually such a one-toy man, but he needed precision tonight without too much bite. He thwapped it lightly against Nicky's testicles. Stretched and weighted as they were, even a light touch was painful; Nicky grunted, stumbled, fell. The rigging caught him, and he scrambled back to his feet and forced his limbs back to their straining stance. Devon rewarded this by striking Nicky's nuts again, upping the force a bit. Perhaps expecting it this time, Nicky kept his feet.

"Now, I do believe we were having a conversation. Tell me what I'm doing."

Another strike. Nicky gasped.

"You're cropping my nuts, sir." Again, and Nicky lifted one foot but quickly put it back, gasping out, "Fuck, it hurts."

Devon knelt down to add a second weight to the leather cord, stretching Nicky's sack a little more. He let it go carefully, stroking one sweat-damp thigh as he released the weight. Nicky's whimper went straight to Devon's cock, but he ignored it. Right now, his boy demanded all his focus.

Devon picked up the crop again and rubbed it against the stretched skin of Nicky's scrotum, then slapped it lightly, several times in succession, until Nicky danced away. "Hold still," Devon warned, grabbing him by the rigging to keep him in place and resuming his tapping with the crop.

It was impressive that Nicky remembered to speak through this treatment. He gritted out, "Tapping my balls, sir," through increasingly heavy breaths that became grunts, then cries: Devon's cue to stop. Devon smoothed over the hot skin with his thumb, gave Nicky's half-hard cock a few quick pumps.

"And I suppose you know what my next question's going to be."

Chest heaving, limbs quaking, Nicky said nothing as Devon worked his erection. Finally, he shook his head, looking contrite and a little frightened. A drop of sweat flew from his chin and plopped to the floor.

Good. Nicky was moving beyond the ability to parse every little thing, moving beyond control and into true subspace. Devon added another weight, and another.

"How do you feel, Nicky?"

"Hurts," he panted.

"How *you* feel, Nicky, not how *it* feels. That's five." Devon wrapped his hands around the stretched skin, radiating heat like a fever, taut and sweaty and, Devon knew, almost unbearably sensitive. Squeezed. Nicky moaned, arched and trembled, his knuckles curling white around his tethers.

"Tired?" was the boy's next try. Devon squeezed harder, added a twist. Nicky screamed, short and sharp, and at the end of it Devon heard one word: "Real!"

"What's that?" Devon leaned in close enough to breathe, literally, down Nicky's neck. He eased his grip on Nicky's balls so the boy could speak.

Nicky slumped forward in the rigging, breathing hard through bared teeth, dripping sweat, legs still spread wide but no longer supporting his weight. Devon didn't think him capable of standing just now, so he let him stay as he was.

"Real," Nicky panted. His eyes were squeezed tight, had been shut the whole time since his outburst. "Pain is real." He scraped his bare feet along the floor, found purchase, heaved himself up again. "Can't ignore it, can't push it away, can't smile and pretend it's something else."

Devon rewarded Nicky's honesty by hooking two more weights onto the rawhide wrap. Nicky threw his head back and growled, arms bending a little at the elbows as his body tensed head to toe.

"That's what you do with everything else, isn't it. Push it away. Ignore it. Pretend. Everything in its own tidy little box and nothing allowed out into the sunshine unless you say so."

"Yes, sir." Even Nicky's voice was trembling now, strained as the rest of him.

"And you hate that. You hate how cold it is, how dead, even as you do it for money every day, whore yourself out to a new audience night after night."

"Y-yes, sir."

Squeezing again. Twisting. Nicky pressed his knees together with a whimper, probably didn't even realize he was doing it. Devon shoved them apart. "Six. Hate it just as much as you hate how easy everything is. How effortlessly powerful you are."

"Y—" Nicky's throat locked. The pain had to be blinding. His feet gave out again, the ropes around his chest biting hard and raising flushed diamonds of flesh between the rigging. "Yes, sir."

"So you come here to give every last thing you have—your pride, your control, your suffering," *squeeze*, "to someone who will take without guilt or question, who will suck you dry and revel in kicking you down."

Beyond speech, Nicky jerked his head, fast and uncoordinated.

Devon relaxed his grip, let the boy catch his breath, and asked, uncertain of the answer for the first time, "Is that all?"

"No," Nicky whispered. "Pain's familiar. Comfortable." A pause, and then, "Dangerous. Scary. Thrilling. A challenge."

Even through the intensity of the moment, this made Devon smile. "All that at once, huh?" He grabbed another weight—up to seven now—clipped it on and said, "Stand up, arms back out."

Nicky took several long seconds to get back to his feet, his face flushing bright pink with the strain as he held his arms out again. He seemed so far lost in the effort, in a sub's ecstasy of agonizing compliance, that Devon wondered if he'd even hear the next question.

"Now tell me. Familiar how?"

"Family," Nicky replied. Devon grabbed Nicky's scrotum and squeezed again. He was hesitant to cause more pain when the boy had already been reduced to one-word answers, but positive reinforcement was critical now. Nicky screamed, short and sharp like last time, a choked, half-formed "*Fuck*!" buried inside. When he could breathe again he added, "Dad, grandpa, uncle Tim. Car crash, all . . . all died. Knew nothing but pain f-for years."

"So you walled off," Devon said softly, giving those abused nuts a tug, making Nicky wail. "Never got close to another man again. And *this*," another tug, another wail, "is your substitute." Silence, save Nicky's ragged breaths. "Except even this is never enough, because you're too afraid of giving up your precious control to experience it the way it's meant to be experienced. Right?"

More silence. Devon tilted up Nicky's scrotum and smacked the bottom of it hard with his bare hand. "Right?"

"Yes!" Nicky cried, "Yes!"

"And let's talk about me for a moment. Why do you think I'm bothering with you and all your fucked-up baggage, huh?"

For a moment, confusion and . . . sadness? disappointment? fear? . . . overwhelmed the pain on Nicky's face. "I . . . I don't know, sir."

Another slap to the scrotum, and Nicky's knees pressed together, trapping Devon's hand.

"Sure you do." Devon wrenched Nicky's legs back open. "You think I want you because you're pretty. A good fuck. Willing. TV's ex-darling and Broadway's shining star. Nicky fucking Avery. Is that right?"

Nicky hesitated, and Devon, unwilling to let him retreat now they'd come so far, gave his nuts another hard slap.

"Yes, sir!" Nicky barked out. "Yes!"

"Well." Devon gripped Nicky's chin with his free hand and tilted his face up. "Look at me, Nicky. Open your eyes."

Nicky obeyed, but blinked them immediately shut again as sweat dripped past his lashes. Devon wiped them with the sleeve of his shirt and then grabbed Nicky by the hair. "Listen to me carefully, boy. This is your last stop. This shit ends here. You can have this"—another hard squeeze to abused nuts, and Nicky's eyes squeezed closed to match but then opened and fixed on Devon's a moment later—"if you want it. You can have it if it thrills you, if it comforts you, if it turns you on, if it frightens and stimulates and challenges you. But not for some ill-conceived notion of guilt, or karma, or any other bullshit 'because I deserve it' thing. And let me tell you something else. I'm not here for *this*." Another squeeze, except this time he wrapped his fingers around Nicky's wilted cock, too. "I can get this anywhere. A pretty face, a tight body, fame, money, obedience—I can have that any time I want, but from you it's not enough. I said that yesterday and I meant it. What I *am* here for is *this*." He gave Nicky's head a hard shake by the hair. "This, Nicky. This is what I want from you. And I promise you I will always treat you like the priceless treasure you are. Do you understand?"

Wide blue eyes, dazed and shaken, burrowed into Devon's, looking for . . . what? Clarification? The lie? The trick? Whatever the case, it was far too much thinking and not nearly enough feeling. Devon tightened his fingers in Nicky's hair and on Nicky's cock and balls, and a choked, mewling cry spilled from Nicky's parted lips.

"Do you understand?"

Devon squeezed tighter, tighter. Waiting.

Tighter.

And *finally*, Nicky burst into tears.

Devon let go, slid his hand up Nicky's torso to his neck, let it rest there for a moment before tilting Nicky forward, guiding the boy's head onto his shoulder. Nicky fell into him, hands reaching out as if to hug Devon before being stopped by their tethers.

"That's it," Devon murmured, running fingers through the damp hair at the nape of Nicky's neck with one hand while reaching behind himself with the other, feeling for the emergency shears he'd left on a nearby shelf. Nicky moaned through his tears as Devon leaned away, and he winced, torn between needing to free Nicky and not wanting to leave him alone, even for a moment, in the fragility of his hard-earned catharsis.

"No," Nicky choked out as Devon stepped away, just for a second, just long enough to reach the shears—ripping off the band-aid instead of pulling slowly. Nicky shook his head, sniffed and rubbed his face against one bare, slick shoulder. But he didn't struggle against the restraints, didn't try to follow Devon those three steps. Too worn down with fighting himself.

Devon grabbed the scissors and rushed back to Nicky's side, placed a hand on one sweaty hip as he squatted down to snip the rawhide strap holding the weights to Nicky's balls. Nicky leaned simultaneously into and away from his touch, and Devon tightened his grip, warning, "Hold on, this won't be fun," as the weights clunked to the floor.

"No," Nicky said again as Devon unwound the rawhide, still not just crying but sobbing, almost too hard to speak, even to breathe, looking so young and broken it stole Devon's breath to remember he'd brought Nicky this far on purpose—shattered the boy with meticulous, deliberate intent.

"It's all right," he said as Nicky tucked his buckling knees together, seeking to ease the pain of reperfusion in his testicles, or maybe to prolong it. Devon stood and pulled Nicky into a hug, rubbed his back and stroked his hair as his tears soaked Devon's shirt.

Wetness pricked Devon's own eyes, but he could ill afford sentimentality now. Nicky was still strung up like a row of Christmas lights, and while *he* might not want the scene to end, Devon knew damn well better what the boy needed.

So he stepped back, forcing himself to ignore Nicky's protest, and cut Nicky's hands free. Nicky wasted no time covering his face with them, didn't even give Devon time to unwind the ropes still wrapped around his wrists. Ashamed of his tears? Or merely too naked for comfort with all those nasty *feelings* dangling out for all the world to see? The second, Devon thought. Hoped.

He wrapped an arm around Nicky and cut through the main support rope. Nicky, sweat-slick and boneless, slid right through Devon's hold and crumpled to the floor. He curled in on himself, cried into his knees.

"Easy now," Devon murmured, kneeling down beside Nicky. "It's okay, I'm here. You did great and I'm not going anywhere, okay?" He took Nicky by the shoulders and sat him up, wrapped both arms around him and hugged him close.

Nicky leaned hard into Devon's embrace and mumbled through tears, "I'm sorry, sir, I'm sorry."

"It's okay, Nicky. Shhh, it's okay. Nothing to be sorry for. You did exactly what you were supposed to."

Nicky rubbed his face against Devon's shoulder, clutched at him with both hands. Devon held on tight and rocked him gently, one hand rubbing circles on Nicky's bare back, the other curling around his head.

"Then why did you—" Nicky snuffled into Devon's chest. "I never, I never called my safeword, I didn't want— I could *take* it, sir!"

"I know you could. But you didn't have to anymore. Look at you, Nicky—look what you've accomplished. Look where you are now; you *trusted* me."

He felt Nicky's head bob against his chest, made out a mumbled "Yes, sir" through the tears.

"No more 'sir' tonight, Nicky. Come back to me now."

"Yes, sir," Nicky said, and damn it all, but he couldn't exactly fault the boy for staying down so deep when he'd taken him by the hand and led him there. Still, it left him uneasy. Had he misread Nicky? Pushed him too hard? God knew he'd hurt the boy for real—beyond his capacity to think, to doubt, even to cope.

But Nicky had wanted that, hadn't he? Needed it, even.

"Come on," he whispered, pressing kisses to the crown of Nicky's head, one after another—an exclamation mark, a question mark, an ellipses. "Come back to me."

Again, he felt Nicky nod against his chest, but the man was still crying. Still clinging. "If you, uh," *sniffle*, "if you meant it, sir."

Whether he'd miscalculated or not seemed beside the point now. Nicky still clearly needed him to *be* sir, so he let the title slide and asked, "Meant what?"

Nicky peeled his fingers from Devon's shirt and held them out, wrists together, by his bowed head. He sniffled again, but the crying, it seemed, was stopping. "What you said, sir. About . . . about keeping me. About wanting me for"—another hitching sniffle—"for *me*."

Phantom bindings loosed from Devon's chest, yet still his relief left him breathless. To know for certain what was going through Nicky's head, why he was still crying, why he was still down so deep. To know he'd done right by Nicky, *more* than right, and Nicky's tears . . . God, were one of the sweetest, most magnificent things he'd ever seen, second only to the expression on Nicky's upturned face—happy and hopeful, raw and exposed and trusting, likely for the first time in his entire adult life. It was . . . He was . . .

"Mine," Devon growled, squeezing tightly enough to make Nicky grunt. "I meant every word. Of course I did." Devon gave in to the urge to pepper Nicky's head with kisses. "Every," kiss, "last," kiss, "word."

Nicky tilted his head back, and Devon's next kiss landed square on his lips. They were salty, flushed, still quivering a little with the remnants of his crying. Devon ravaged them, drawing them between his teeth, sucking Nicky's tongue into his mouth, driving his own deep into Nicky's.

He sensed Nicky's need to be claimed now, to be offered proof of his promise. But he also wanted to remind Nicky of the other half of that promise, of the part he knew now for certain had been absent from Nicky's past encounters: *I will always treat you like the priceless treasure you are.*

So he wrapped one hand around both of Nicky's wrists and pulled him to the floor, laying him on his back at Devon's knees. "Hush now," he said, tightening his hold on the boy's wrists until he was certain it hurt just how it had their first night, just how Nicky liked it. He leaned over and wiped the tears from Nicky's cheeks, the gentleness a stark contrast to his crushing grip. "Close your eyes."

Nicky sniffled once more, and obeyed.

"Now tell me you're mine."

Even through closed lids, Devon could see the light dancing in Nicky's eyes. "I'm yours, Sir."

Devon smiled fiercely at the audible change of tone—he could *hear* that capital S. "Tell me you belong to me."

A watery smile spread across Nicky's lips. "I belong to you, Sir."

Devon spit into his free hand and wrapped it around Nicky's flaccid cock, avoiding the tender scrotum as he began to pump. The flesh firmed quickly in his grip. "Tell me you're the luckiest boy alive."

"I am the *luckiest* boy in the whole world, Sir."

Devon bent down and sucked Nicky's half-hard length into his mouth, biting softly and humming around the erection as it sprang to life against his tongue. He scraped his teeth from root to tip and pulled back to blow warm air across the head, then sank back down, swallowing him balls deep.

Nicky arched up beneath him and moaned, "*Fuck*, Sir, the luckiest boy alive!"

Under the circumstances, Devon thought he could excuse the boy for speaking out of turn.

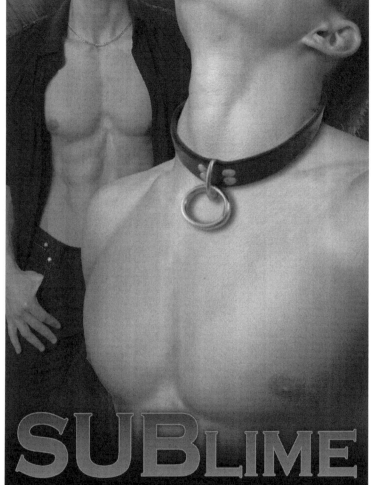

SUBLIME
COLLECTED SHORTS
BY RACHEL HAIMOWITZ

SUBLIME

COLLECTED SHORTS

(MASTER CLASS, #2)

RACHEL HAIMOWITZ

RIPTIDE
PUBLISHING

To Amara, for all the claymores and hand grenades, and for helping to make the Riptide launch so very special.

ALL-NIGHTER

I have pulled all-nighters more times in my life than I can count—study sessions in college, night shoots through five seasons of *Prey*, a few too many after-parties. I'm used to it, occasionally thrive on it. I'm even good at it, one of the few of my contemporaries who can still go five or six days on just a few hours' sleep.

But never until tonight had I looked forward to it with quite such . . . zeal.

Sir had been warning—promising, teasing—the whole damn week that I'd better get my sleep, because once Sunday night rolled around, there'd be no time for such frivolities. I got out of the matinee around seven, grabbed a quick bite, and came home to a note on the door that said simply, "Strip." So I shed my clothes right there in the foyer, settled on my heels, laid my hands palms-up on my widespread knees, and waited.

And waited. And waited.

I'm still waiting, but that's okay. I know he'll come soon. In the meantime, I distract myself with the chill of the apartment, with the hardness of the tile floor beneath my knees, with delicious thoughts of what he will do to me—or, if I'm a very lucky slave, what he will allow me to do to him—when finally he deigns me worthy of his attention. I know I mustn't fall asleep, though the pull grows strong as the hours stretch. I know I mustn't touch myself, though my cock aches with need at the slightest thought of him.

When at last he comes, I do not hear him. I do not even see him. One moment there is cold and hardness and a world filled with him inside my head, and the next there is warmth and softness and his chest to my back in the real world, his arms around my waist, his lips on my neck and his breath in my ear. I gasp my surprise, moan my pleasure, melt back into him and shudder with the force of my need.

"What a good boy you are," he rumbles near my shoulder, follows it with a bite that makes me hiss even as the knowledge that he's praising me, marking me, *claiming* me makes me glow. "Do you know how long you waited for me?" Another bite, gentler, soothed immediately after by a lick, a suck, a kiss. "Do you know how long you kneeled there, naked, cold, resisting sleep?"

"No, Sir," I breathe, unable to find my voice as one of his hands presses flat and tight to my stomach and the other snakes down between my legs. His lips work my shoulder, my neck, my ear, while his hand works my balls, my cock, spreading tingling warmth and bright white sparks of pleasure from my toes to the tips of my hair. The sensations meet in the middle, coil tight in my belly beneath his hand. I moan again, bite down on my lip and clutch at my thighs to keep them still, to stop myself from thrusting into his fist.

"Five hours," he whispers, his tongue following the words, making its own vibrations across the shell of my left ear. *God, no wonder I'm so stiff.* "You waited five hours for this"—he squeezes my cock and pulls, just the way he knows will drive me crazy—"and this"—a soft bite to the corded tendon of my neck, a hot sweep of tongue across the skin pinched between his teeth—"and this"—a jut of hips, his hard cock pressing against my ass, promising the wild heights of pleasure to which only he can take me. "You waited all night for me. Such a good boy," he purrs. "*Such* a *good boy.*"

He stands then, his cloak of warmth falling away, and it's all I can do not to follow him, to cling to his leg, to whimper my protest at the loss. But then he puts his hand out and says, "Five hours 'til daybreak. And I plan to break *you* at least three times between now and then."

This time I cannot hold back the whimper as he takes my hand and pulls me to my feet. For a moment he has to hold me there, my knees weak from my long night of immobility and the mere *thought* of so many orgasms.

As he guides me to our bedroom, binds my hands and feet to the bedposts with soft well-worn leather and thoughtfully fingers his selection of favorite paddles and crops, I squirm with anticipation and habitual mischief—has there ever been a bond I haven't tested, even when the last thing I want is to escape?—and think to myself, Best. All-nighter. Ever.

DOWN IN THE WOODSHOP

Nicky pressed his ear to the door of the storage unit Devon had rented in Park Slope, trying to hear what was going on inside. Nothing, as far as he could tell. But he knew Devon was in there—Devon had said he'd be there, and the man had never lied to him.

He decided to knock, but didn't wait for a reply before entering. The first thing to hit him was the smell: sawdust and metal. The next was the sight of a very startled Devon, blinking toward the open door and looking as if Nicky had just snuck up behind him with an air horn.

"What are you doing here?" Devon asked, clearly surprised but also, Nicky thought, kind of pleased to see him.

Nicky closed the door and looked around the little storage space Devon had turned into a woodshop. "Thought I'd come by and see what you were doing down here that you obviously love more than me, what with the constantly leaving me for it."

Devon chuckled at Nicky's fake pout and held his arms out for a hug, but Nicky folded his arms across his chest.

"Uh uh," Devon warned, stepping forward and hugging Nicky anyway, right around his crossed arms. "Don't you make that face at me. What if I said I was making something *for you*?"

Damn the man for playing him so well. "Really?"

"Well," Devon hedged, kissing Nicky on the nose, "No, not really."

Nicky muttered a good-natured "Figures" and pushed Devon away, heading toward the workbench along the back wall to see what was *really* going on over there.

But he only made it one step before Devon grabbed him by the elbow and said, "Uh uh. Off limits."

"You're so full of shit," Nicky laughed, pulling his arm free and heading toward the bench again. "Lemme see."

He got two steps closer this time—halfway there, as small as the room was—before Devon stopped him again. "You don't know how to listen, do you?"

"I—" Nicky's snarky comment died on his lips when he saw the look on Devon's face. No, not Devon's face; *Sir's* face.

"You want to be over there so bad? Fine. But you'll at least be useful." Devon grabbed Nicky by the wrist and dragged him the last few feet to the workbench, which was so cluttered with tools and scraps and things Nicky couldn't make heads or tails of that he didn't know where to begin. Beside the bench was half a shelving unit; even in its infancy, Nicky could tell it would be stunning. He couldn't possibly help with something like that.

"I don't know how—"

"I know," Sir said. He gave Nicky a hard shove against the bench and gathered the hem of Nicky's shirt in his hands. Nicky lifted his arms without thought or instruction, letting Sir strip him. "So shut up and be pretty while *I* work."

Sir perched himself on a stool, picked up a tiny file and an intricately cut wood panel, and set to work.

Nicky waited for Sir to touch him, to turn eyes to him, to pay him even the slightest mind. Alas, he did not. Not that Nicky had really expected him to, though, not after he'd barged into Sir's private space like a spoiled child demanding attention. Besides, this wasn't the first time Sir had ignored him, and surely would not be the last.

But in all their time together, Nicky had never quite learned how to endure that. Or maybe he just didn't feel like behaving today . . . At least not without a little discipline first.

When he grew tired of watching Sir work (a whole ninety seconds in, maybe ninety-five), Nicky let his eyes, and then his hands, stray back to the workbench. He fiddled with a rasp, then something he thought might be an awl, and then ran a piece of sandpaper lightly over the back of his hand.

Without looking up from his work, Sir snatched it away. "Stop touching things."

Nicky mumbled an apology and scratched at his hand, which itched now where he'd rubbed it with the sandpaper.

Sir slapped his fingers. "Hold still."

"Sorry," he said again, folding his hands in front of him. He'd yet to say "Sir," and so far he'd not been called on that. Maybe Devon really didn't want to play. Or maybe he'd been Sir from the moment Nicky had walked in, and simply didn't feel like Nicky deserved the spanking he was after. Maybe he was just letting Nicky dig a hole too deep to climb out of.

Nicky had to admit, that thought held appeal.

He grabbed onto the edge of the workbench, leaned his weight on his arms, and dug yet deeper. "Is there another stool?" he asked.

Sir turned the piece of wood in his hand, filing down the edge of a curlicue that didn't seem to need filing. "No."

"Oh."

Sir finished with the piece he was holding and swapped it for another one. Nicky flexed his fingers on the bench and shifted his weight from his left foot to his right. The quiet, broken only by the *swwf swwf swwf* of Sir's meticulous filing, was killing him.

"Got a radio in here?"

Swwf swwf swwf. "Yes."

But Sir made no move to turn it on or show Nicky where it was. *Swwf swwf swwf.* Nicky focused on Sir's fingers, on those giant, powerful hands doing such tiny, delicate work. His own hands itched to move, and when he couldn't hold them back anymore, he reached for the curlicued panel Sir had just finished filing.

Sir sprang to his feet, threw down the wood and the file in his hand, and grabbed Nicky's wrist, squeezing until Nicky dropped the panel. "Damn it, boy," he growled, "Haven't you learned yet to *hold still*?"

Nicky knew better than to answer. He dropped his eyes to the floor and waited for whatever would come next, hissed as Sir slammed his hand against the workbench.

"I can't believe I have to restrain you," Sir growled, grabbing a staining rag with his free hand and balling it into Nicky's upturned palm. "I can't take you anywhere, can I?"

For a moment, Nicky resented that. Just because he was being bad on purpose now didn't mean he *couldn't* behave. But of course Sir knew that; he was just playing the game Nicky wanted to play. Nicky should be grateful—*was* grateful—that Sir was a considerate enough master to do that for him.

God, how Nicky loved him.

Sir let go of Nicky's wrist and snapped, "Don't move. Think you can handle that for five seconds?"

Nicky froze. He even held his breath, determined to do what Sir had asked of him to the very best of his ability. Yet his thoughts were whirring; just moments ago he'd been goading Sir, but now his whole world had narrowed down to the desire to please the man. How did Sir *do* that to him?

He decided he didn't care. Thinking was entirely too much work now, anyway. He'd just sit back, relax, let Sir do whatever he—

Sir picked up a c-clamp and stuck it over Nicky's hand.

"Wh—what are you doing?"

Sir ignored him, continued to wind the clamp closed. He didn't really intend to—? "Sir?" Nicky asked, unable to hide the fear in his voice.

"Be quiet," Sir said, calm as a breezeless day. The clamp touched the rag in Nicky's palm. He couldn't help it—he pulled his hand away.

Sir glowered at him, mouth open in outrage, and said, "Put. It. Back."

Nicky wanted to, he really did. *Anything* to get Sir to stop looking at him like that, like he'd let him down, like he'd *failed* him. But . . .

Sir put down the clamp, grabbed Nicky's head in both hands, and kissed him. "I love you," he whispered in one ear. Another breath-stealing, blood-rushing kiss, and then, "Trust me," he whispered in the other.

Though Nicky couldn't stop his hand from trembling, he slid it back onto the table, palm up, just like before. Sir replaced the rag and began to turn the clamp again. He watched Nicky carefully, eyes darting between the clamp and Nicky's face.

At first there was only pressure. Then pain, but not too much. Nicky tugged and discovered he could pull away if he tried. He turned his eyes up to Sir's and then back down again, and Sir tightened the clamp some more, until he pulled a little whimper from Nicky.

Nicky grimaced and tried to flex his fingers, found he could barely move them and only at great expense. One hard, gasp-inducing tug made it clear that he was well and truly stuck.

"Good," Sir whispered, drawing the word out into a caress, bending down and sucking one of Nicky's trapped knuckles into his mouth. Nicky groaned, found his free hand wandering to Sir's hair.

"Ah ah ah," Sir warned, bringing one hand up to the bulge forming in Nicky's jeans and wrapping the other around Nicky's wrist. "Sit perfectly still; only *I* may dance."

Nicky laughed—only *Sir* would quote the *Simpsons* at a time like this—then moaned as Sir squeezed his erection before freeing it from the confines of his boxers and pants. No skin-to-skin contact, though; Sir let it bob there in the air, grinning as Nicky groaned again. He grabbed another rag and another c-clamp off the workbench and secured Nicky's other hand.

"There," Sir sighed, stepping back and taking in the picture he'd made: Nicky topless, his cock hanging out of his pants, both hands pinned to the table, the strain of steady but endurable pain creasing his brows and parting his lips.

Sir flicked the tip of Nicky's cock with his thumb and forefinger and leaned forward to kiss him again, then grabbed his little file and the piece of sandpaper Nicky had played with earlier. "Well," he said, "I guess you're my new project, after all."

That settled it. Nicky was going to have to start interrupting Sir way, *way* more often.

STAINLESS STEEL

The table is hard and cold against Nicky's bare skin. Stainless steel, like an operating room. The mirror on the ceiling bounces light, too bright, as cold and hard as the table beneath him. He could probably turn his head, avoid the glare if he tried, but he doesn't.

Stainless steel around his ankles and wrists, binding his legs straight, his arms above his head. His limbs are stretched too far, too tight; the cuffs bite into the tops of his feet, the bones beneath his thumbs. It is a cold, hard pain. The mirror reflects this, too.

When Sir finally enters the room—quiet, so quiet that Nicky doesn't notice until he sees Sir in the mirror, standing by his head— Nicky is shivering and sore, struggling a little, so far lost in the hard and the cold, in the shine of stainless steel, that he can hardly be bothered to remember his own name. No matter—he doesn't need one here anyway.

"Good," Sir whispers, his hand coming up to stroke a line down Nicky's jaw, Nicky's neck, across one shoulder and to his chest. Even Sir's hand gleams, his finger— No, not his flesh. A knife. Stainless steel. Sir holds it before him, and in the flat of the blade Nicky sees the stark reflection of his own fear.

The knife disappears from view, and its edge scrapes like a shaving razor across Nicky's chest, tugging at hairs, skimming a nipple. He arches and gasps, steel biting into his ankles and wrists, pulse pounding against those gleaming restraints.

Sir's free hand presses into Nicky's sternum. "Be still," he orders. The tip of the knife digs in next to Sir's hand, a stainless steel complement to his flesh, his power.

Nicky closes his eyes against the thrill, the pain, and manages to hold mostly still; only his fingers disobey, curling into fists. When he opens his eyes again, he sees a single bead of blood reflected in the mirror. He sees his cock, long hard, twitch against his thigh.

"No," Sir says. His hands reach between Nicky's legs, pinch his scrotum. Nicky wills his erection to fade. Sir helps by pinching harder, too hard even for Nicky. A gleam of steel at his groin, and Nicky holds his breath, bites back a whimper. He cannot stop it from escaping when he feels the chill of steel against his softening cock, but Sir shushes him, strokes his thigh. "Open your eyes," he says. "Look," he says.

Nicky obeys, seeking his reflection in the mirror. A glint of steel between his legs, but not the knife. Just a gates of hell, cold and hard, and Sir's deft fingers strapping it in place. Nicky's filling it already. A different kind of pleasure-pain. Another whimper.

Sir's hand strokes low on his belly, pressing hard, holding him down. Soft and warm and nothing at all like the knife that follows, scraping a shallow pattern into his flesh. Hot, burning, like Sir's eyes, hard steel flashing in the light. He knows what Sir etches into him even without looking, knows what Sir has written. One single word in stainless steel:

Mine.

PRETTY

"**P**retty," they tell me. It's always fucking "pretty." The prettyboy actor, the pretty lips, the pretty cheekbones. I suppose they could call me worse things, like "hack" or "fraud," but it sure would be nice to be called "talented" or "hardworking" every once in a while.

Sir doesn't seem to mind it, though, when it's the media, an article, a fan site. Takes pride in it, even, when it's some nameless, faceless voice that will never, as he says, get to see the Pretty up close. But in this Vegas club, where at least a dozen men have approached in the span of an hour with the expert pick-up line "Well hey there, Pretty" (or some minor variation) while we were trying to get smashed in peace, when half of them stole a touch and one even tried to drag me to the dance floor before Sir laid a heavy, unmistakably menacing hand on the guy's arm, it really began to get under his skin. Never mind that men were hitting on him jut as often as on me, that people were asking him for pictures and autographs. He wasn't the one who belonged to me, after all; *I* belonged to *him*.

Sir transferred that menacing hand to my own arm and plucked my half-finished drink from my fingers. "Time to go," he said, in a tone that brooked no argument. I nodded mutely and dropped my eyes, excitement coiling in my belly. Clearly he wanted to play, and I . . . well, I just *wanted*.

Out into the street, Sir clutching my wrist hard enough to bruise. He dragged me as I hustled to keep up with his larger, more decisive, considerably less drunken steps. Through a lobby, into an elevator, down a hall . . . I didn't know where we were, didn't care. All that mattered was getting to our room or, hell, *any* room.

"Strip," Sir ordered the instant we got inside. I obeyed with all the eagerness I could manage in my current uncoordinated state and waited to be told to kneel, or bend, or—

"Wait."

Well, that was different.

"Stand there. Don't move. I'll be back."

And then he left me, naked and alone, flush and aroused, waiting patiently the way only subs really could.

An hour passed, but I never moved from the spot Sir had placed me in. I didn't even touch myself. Not once. I was tired and tipsy and I'd gone soft, but when Sir returned with a plastic shopping bag and saw the smile on my face, I knew he knew right away that I'd behaved.

"Very good, Pretty." "Good" was full of approval and love, but he spat "Pretty" like an expletive, jealous and lustful. "I bought you something. Hate for all that pretty to go to waste." He thrust the bag at my chest and said, "Take it. Put it on." Slapped me once, lightly, across the face—painless, a warning—and added, "Don't even think of arguing."

My pulse pounded in my buzzing ears as I opened the bag, my cock raging hard again, my mind tripping with possibilities. It was too big and soft to be a new toy, but maybe it was a pair of leather pants, or one of those bondage shirts, or . . .

. . . Or a dress?

Pink.

Chiffon.

"Go on, Pretty," Sir said again. And though surely I was flushing as pink as the dress, I pulled it over my head and turned so Sir could zip me. The arms and shoulders were too tight, not meant for muscle like mine. I couldn't quite fill out the bust. Lace dangled from the sleeve cuffs and tickled my thumbs.

I wondered if I was the first person in history to tent this particular dress with a raging hard-on.

Sir eyed me like a particularly fine dessert. His gaze dropped to my cock and he snatched out a hand, grabbed the skirt and yanked it up past my waist. He covered my face with a mass of pink chiffon and pushed me back until I fell onto the bed.

"Pretty," he growled again, shoving two fingers into his mouth and then into my ass, bending over to mash a biting kiss against my lips as he prepped me with one stroke, two, before pulling his hand out and replacing it with his cock. It hurt in all the right ways and I arched and writhed beneath him as he cried, "Pretty, pretty, pretty!" in time to his thrusts: half drunken sneer, half growl, all pure animal lust. "But you're *my* pretty, Nicky. Say it!"

"Your pretty, Sir."

"Again!"

"I'm *your* pretty, Sir!"

He nudged the lace collar aside and bit down hard on my collarbone, shoved the skirt up to wrap a hand around my cock and pump. He was close already, his hips snapping hard and out of synch, his eyes boring into mine and brimming with possessive need. "Come for me, Pretty," he growled. "Now."

And really, who was I to argue with my master? But I think I might have ruined my pretty new dress.

MILK RUN

"**H**oney, I'm home!" Nicky shouted in an eye-rolling singsong as he tossed his coat and messenger bag on the couch and locked the door behind him. Sir emerged from his study a moment later to give Nicky a kiss and a hug; he didn't know he was Sir yet, but he would soon.

Sir stepped back, hands still resting loose and affectionate on Nicky's arms, and said, "Hey, I thought you were stopping for milk."

Nicky feigned surprise, then contrition. "Oh! I forgot." He pasted on his best "I'm too cute to stay angry at" face and said, "Oops?"

Sir pouted, actually pouted—and didn't that just kill Nicky every time—and folded his arms across his chest with a distinct air of petulance. "What am I supposed to put in my cornflakes in the morning?"

Nicky had a few salty (*ha ha*) words on that subject, but rather than voice them, he let them gleam in his eyes and said, "I'm sorry, Sir," through a smile he had to drop his head to hide.

Sir caught the cue instantly, his disappointment blinking away, anger taking its place. His big hands returned to Nicky's arms and squeezed, painfully tight. "Too careless to remember, or just too lazy?"

Nicky knew it wasn't a question he was expected to answer. Sir shook him hard and pushed him to the floor. Once he was down, Sir stepped on his chest.

Nicky was still grinning like an idiot, but luckily Sir had turned without noticing and left for the dungeon. By the time he returned, Nicky had managed to wipe the smile off his face, despite having had the audacity to pick himself up and sprawl across the much more comfortable couch.

Sir stopped short at the sight of Nicky on the furniture, anger darkening and hardening his face. He came at Nicky with such an air of menace that Nicky actually thought, *Oh shit!* and shrank back against the couch, but he wasn't fast enough to avoid Sir's hand, which connected with his cheek hard enough to knock him back to the floor.

Through lips that suddenly felt three sizes too big—though surely they were not; Sir would never harm him—Nicky smiled.

His jeans suddenly felt three sizes too small.

Sir yanked Nicky's head up by the hair and shoved a large black rubber strap-on against his lips. "Open," Sir said, so of course Nicky did, and Sir thrust the cock straight down his throat. Sir was still holding his hair, so he couldn't get away, not even as his gag reflex brought tears to his eyes.

Sir murmured, "Through your nose, Nicky. That's it, breathe," as Nicky gagged around the dildo, tears streaming down his cheeks. "Breathe, Nicky," Sir said again, much sterner this time, and Nicky realized he hadn't been. He forced himself still and sucked a wet, shaky breath in through his nose.

Sir nodded, released his hold on Nicky's hair and petted him. He didn't fasten the straps, but he only let go of the dildo after warning, "Don't drop it."

The urge to spit it out or, heck, throw it up, was nearly overwhelming, but Sir was watching him, eyes narrowed, just daring him to disobey, to disappoint. Nicky would not. He nodded once and peeled his lips back from his teeth so Sir could see that he was using them to keep the cock in place.

"Good boy. That's good," Sir said. And then, "Chin up." Nicky tilted his head back, and Sir fastened a collar around his neck. By the feel of it, it wasn't the one Nicky usually wore, the one he'd worked so hard to earn. This was smaller, lighter, more discreet. When Sir was done buckling it on, Nicky heard a little padlock click into place. Then Sir's hand was back in front of Nicky's mouth, and he said, "Give it to me."

Nicky didn't need to be told twice to spit that massive cock out. He coughed, ran his tongue over numb lips as Sir held the dildo by the straps, the thick black cock dangling before him, glistening with Nicky's saliva.

Sir turned his eyes from the dildo to Nicky and said, "Ass up, boy."

That damn sneaky smile returned as Nicky dropped his pants and bent over, spread his legs and grabbed his ankles just like Sir had taught him. But this time, he forgot to hide the grin before he turned his back.

"You dirty little whore," Sir drawled, clearly amused, landing a heavy smack on Nicky's ass as Nicky presented it to him. "Look how eager you are. You want this cock, don't you?"

"Yes, Sir." Nicky couldn't help it; Sir could probably *hear* the damn smile in his voice.

"You won't be smiling in a minute, boy."

Sir slapped Nicky again, a dozen times in rapid succession, stopping only to wrap an arm around Nicky's waist when Nicky's squirming yelps made it hard for Sir to aim.

"Don't fight me," Sir warned, starting up again, his heavy hand landing over and over on the same patch of burning skin.

When Nicky started yelling for real, Sir let up but did not let Nicky go, and a moment later he was burying that big black dildo in Nicky's ass.

Nicky cried out, arched up against Sir with such force that Sir nearly dropped him. They both ended up on the floor, Nicky on his elbows and knees, forehead pressed to his clenched fists, Sir squatting beside him with one arm around his waist and the other forcing the dildo in deep. Nicky couldn't stop himself from trying to push it out; with no warning, no preparation, and all that tension from the spanking, the pain was just as big as the cock itself.

"No," Sir said softly but with unarguable force, his hands commanding but gentle as they caressed Nicky's ass, the corded muscles in his back. "Just relax. Breathe."

For the second time tonight, Nicky realized he'd forgotten that most basic of necessities. He sucked in a shuddering breath, then another, trying to relax around that invading rubber force. Sir's hands left his body and he whimpered, pushed back, seeking contact, but Sir said, "No. Hold still."

Sir's hands returned, fastening the dildo in place by wending its straps around Nicky's waist and thighs. Again, Nicky heard the click of a little padlock.

Sir rocked up on his heels and deposited himself on the couch, resting his arms along the back. Now it was his turn to smile, if one could give such a title to that self-satisfied smirk. "Get dressed, Nicky."

Nicky stood carefully, wincing the whole time, not yet adjusted to the weight and fullness. Bending over to pull his jeans up made the cock shift. It bumped him just right and his own cock jumped, heedless of—or more likely because of—the pain. The dildo was buried all the way to the narrow little flange at the end, so Nicky's jeans pulled on smooth.

Sir was eyeing Nicky like he wished it were *his* cock splitting Nicky in half. But he sat perfectly still as he asked, "Why'd I do this to you, Nicky?"

"Because I forgot your milk, Sir?"

Sir shrugged and said, "Sure, why not." They both knew the real answer was *Because I can*, or *Because it pleases me*, or even *Because you wanted it*, but an excuse never hurt. "You want to please me, don't you, Nicky?"

Nicky nodded so fast he felt like a bobble-head. "Oh yes, Sir. More than anything."

"Good. Go get me my milk, then."

"L-like this, Sir?"

Sir nodded, his smirk growing wider by the second. Nicky took a tentative step toward the couch, where his coat still lay, and gasped again, this time with a little more pleasure than pain. His arousal was obvious through his skin-hugging jeans. Another step. He began to think he might almost be able to walk as if he didn't have a giant dick shoved up his ass, though even the slightest motion sent little jolts from the fake cock to his real one.

When Nicky reached out for his coat, Sir caught his wrist in one big hand. "No," he said again. He'd been saying that a lot tonight. He reached up to adjust Nicky's slave collar, tucking it mostly beneath his shirt collar. "Go without it."

Nicky nodded and Sir released him. As Nicky fished his keys from his pocket and walked-shuffled-waddled through the door, the smile crept back onto his face. This time, he didn't care *who* saw it.

TOO MUCH

Nicky could no longer distinguish his left hand from his right. They were tied behind his back, snug together, wrapped in several coils of nylon rope that snaked their way up his forearms and pinned his elbows nearly together just below his shoulder blades. They weren't numb, no . . . that would be too easy. Not cold but hot, two burning lumps of flame twined into one, pulsing and writhing up his arms.

It would be even worse later, of course, when Sir would tug that one magic end on his rigging and send the whole of it spilling to the floor, restoring full circulation. Nicky would be free of his bindings then, but still trapped—by the weakness of his oxygen-starved limbs, by the pain of fresh perfusion, by Sir's foot on his chest or the weight of Sir's stare or Sir's simple, unspoken command: *Be still until I say otherwise.*

Now, though, Nicky couldn't move if he wanted to. He'd tried, of course, tried for the better part of . . . of . . . How long had Sir left him here, the balls of his feet barely touching the floor, the spreader bar clipped to the shackles on his ankles forcing his stance too wide for either balance or comfort, his chest and shoulders and arms nearly shrieking with the strain of their bondage. He was flexible, but this . . . Sir had set out to make him sweat, and Sir was never, ever less than perfect at that sort of thing. At *anything,* Nicky mentally corrected. Never less than perfect at *anything.*

Time passed funny when you were blindfolded and gagged. Sir had even made him wear earplugs. Nicky didn't mind; he liked them, in fact. Liked that Sir had found a way to own even those orifices too small for anything else. Wished only that Sir were here to claim him in person, to bear witness to the suffering Nicky was enduring for him. Not, of course, that Sir didn't own him wholly, even when he wasn't here.

Nicky bit down hard on the leather gag between his teeth and let the muscles in his calves relax ("let" being perhaps too strong a word; he was in control of nothing here, not even himself, and certainly not the burning muscles in his legs). The rope tied above his elbows took his weight. It was attached to the hoist in the ceiling, but also to the coil of rope around his neck, which pulled just tight enough for discomfort when his feet gave out. That pain was nearly lost, though, beneath the cramping agony in his shoulders, and he whimpered through the gag, squeezed his eyes closed behind the blindfold and struggled to make his toes take his weight once again.

His feet obliged, but only for half a minute or so. And then he was suspended from Sir's rigging again, pain ripping through him in waves he could *taste*, like sweat and come and well-oiled leather. *Too much*, he thought, and Sir hadn't even touched him yet.

Sir. Nicky wished he were here to see this. What a picture he would make for Sir now, straining and whimpering, naked and sweat-damp and trapped in a web so intricate that even he knew it turned him into art. A sculpture, a fresco for Sir. A cherished possession, coveted and loved, even when Sir wasn't there to admire it. Yes. Cherished and loved. Nicky ceased his struggling and let the pain wash through him. Pushed through the first wall and felt that familiar rush, that high unlike anything else in the world. Sir would be pleased.

Nicky was getting hard.

Back onto his toes. Ten seconds, fifteen. He counted to the rhythm of his heart, beating faster than normal but not yet pounding. Only Sir could set his heart pounding. Twenty seconds, twenty-one, and his toes gave out again. He slumped against the rigging with a harsh cry. Too much ... *too much*. He needed Sir. He needed—

No. He would not call for him. Not yet. He would not give in or misbehave now, though he'd done much of that in the past. Far too much. Now was the time to prove himself worthy to be owned by such a man. He would endure this for Sir.

Back on his toes. Ten seconds. Twelve. Thirteen before he slipped again, this time screaming around the gag, panting furiously through his nose and squeezing tears from his eyes. He couldn't do it; he couldn't get up again, and hanging here would kill him. He needed ... He *needed*—

Fingers pulled the plugs from his ears and he startled at the unexpected touch, the rush of sound, screamed again as he jarred his shoulders.

"Shhh, it's all right," Sir whispered, stroking his hair, the side of his face, reaching strong hands beneath his arms and hauling him upright. He no longer had the strength to stand, couldn't think around the pain, and when those warm arms cradled him he drooped against Sir's chest, weeping onto Sir's shoulder. *Too much,* he whimpered into the gag, but it came out muffled, nothing but another moan. And then, *For you. Anything for you.*

That came out muffled too, but Sir said, "I know, Nicky, I know," as deft fingers unbuckled the gag. Before he could draw his first real breath in what must have been at least half an hour, Sir was claiming his mouth for himself, driving his tongue where the gag had been just moments before, his taste swirling with the agony of Nicky's bondage, sweetening it through and through. When Sir breathed into his lips, Nicky inhaled deep, accepting the gift.

Then Sir gave him a second gift, just as precious as the first: he stepped back, removed the blindfold, and let Nicky see him. The lights were dim—a kindness to his hypersensitive eyes—but not nearly so much that Nicky couldn't drink in the sight of Sir's naked flesh.

"Thank you, Sir," he whispered, tight and teary, his voice wet with worship and pain. Sir unhanded him, and the ropes took his weight again, but this time he bore it quietly and proud, silent tears mingling with cold sweat, eyes locked on Sir's feet. He could feel Sir's gaze dancing up and down his body like caressing fingers, Sir's pleasure at the artwork he'd created. Even, dare Nicky think it, Sir's pride at his service.

Yet still, the word "Please" escaped the weakness of Nicky's flesh and hung out there between them, too late to take back.

Toes scraping the ground, Nicky chanced one horrified, shameful glance at Sir's face, and was shocked to discover him smiling.

"I'm sorry, Sir," he whispered, though the effort to grit the words out through the pain took almost more than he had to give.

A touch then, a hand cupping the side of his face. He pressed his cheek into Sir's palm and closed his eyes.

"Don't be, Nicky. You've done so well." And then, the ultimate prize, "You've pleased me."

The hand stayed at his cheek, stroking gently, but Sir made no move to free him.

"Look at me," Sir said instead. Nicky obliged, holding his breath as he raised his eyes to Sir's. For a moment, all else was forgotten. For a moment, there was no pain. "Where are you now, Nicky. Tell me."

"In . . ." Nicky licked at quivering lips. "In you."

Sir smiled—a hungry, predatory thing, smug and owning. He stepped closer, pressing his body to Nicky's, and the hand on Nicky's face snaked down his neck and over his shoulder to give the rigging holding him upright a little tug. Nicky jerked back and sobbed out a cry.

"Should I free you of me, then?" Another tug, another cry. Nicky knew Sir's hand was on that magic end, that one hard pull would end it all.

"N-no," he panted. "P-please, no Sir."

Head back, eyes closed, Nicky startled as Sir's teeth latched onto the exposed tendon of his neck. Wet lips, hard suction, hot tongue . . . his moan this time was at least half pleasure, made all the sweeter and sharper by the contrasting pain. His cock twitched, hardening against Sir's thigh. He pushed surreptitiously, wanting more contact; he might not grow fully erect now, not while the pain was this bad, but he could seek to temper it, to give it some balance.

"Ah ah ah," Sir rumbled against his neck, giving the rope in his hand another jerk.

Nicky barked a harsh, teary "Please!" and his feet gave out beneath him.

"Please what?" Sir asked—nay, *demanded*—grabbing Nicky by the chin and jerking his head up. Nicky had nothing to say to that; it was a slip, his second in as many minutes, so he hung there silently, lips quivering, eyes on Sir's chest.

Sir stepped back and studied him in silence. Nicky fell and stood and fell and stood again as Sir watched.

"You look tired," Sir finally said.

"Yes, Sir."

Nicky fell once more and Sir asked again, "Where are you now, Nicky?" When Nicky didn't answer right away, Sir slapped him hard enough to heat his cheek and said, calm as ever, "Look at me. Where are you now? Tell me."

Nicky dredged up the strength to bring his eyes to Sir's, and found in them a kernel of concern surrounded by hunger, by poise, by possession.

"I . . ."

Sir's eyes hardened. He took Nicky by the chin again and barked, "Say it if you need to say it, boy! There's no shame in it, you know that."

He *did* know that. He hadn't always, but he knew it now; it was one of the first lessons Sir had taught him, and Nicky owed him more for that than he could say. Still, he wasn't ready for this to end yet. He shook his head. "No, Sir!"

"Then I think I'd like to decorate you, if you don't mind. Or," Sir said, eyebrow quirking, "even if you do mind. You are a lovely thing, you know. Truly exquisite." He turned toward a shelf full of toys as Nicky flushed warm at the praise. "But you'd be lovelier still in these, don't you think?"

Sir held up a thirty-clothespin zipper, each one black and rubber-tipped and tightened special just for this. Nicky whimpered and squirmed and closed his eyes, thinking, *Too much, too much.* Wondering where he'd find the next high, the key to the next wall, the strength that would stop him from falling.

And knew the instant Sir touched him that everything he needed—everything he'd *ever* need—was in those talented, loving, perfect hands.

A HAIRY SITUATION

"*O*w, damn it!"

Nicky squirmed on the St. Andrews cross, pulling at his bonds but getting nowhere, of course. He'd have been disappointed if he had.

"You just keep talking, Nicky," Sir said through a smirk, grabbing another pubic hair—this one on Nicky's left nut—between thumb and forefinger and yanking it out. Nicky's hips jerked as far as the rope around his waist would let them.

"*Ow!*"

"What's the matter, baby?" *Yoink.* "You don't like this?" *Yoink* again—two at once this time. Nicky's balls tried to crawl up into his belly and his hands curled into fists. He struggled to close his legs, couldn't.

"You know I don't, S—*ow!*—Sir." He spat the name like an invective, which of course earned him . . . "Aah!" This time near the cleft of his ass, three in rapid succession. "Please!"

Sir straightened up, found a single gray hair near Nicky's nipple, and yanked it free. "Would you rather I spanked you, instead?"

"Yes!"

"Whipped you?"

"Yes!"

"Caned you?"

"*Yes!*" Oh *God*, yes.

Another hair, this time from Nicky's armpit, and then Sir walked over to a nearby shelf, his fingers trailing lovingly over a collection of toys. Nicky followed with his eyes, holding his breath. Hoping.

"What about this?" Sir asked, his fingers settling on a violet wand.

Nicky had to think about that one for a second, but he finally said, "Yes, Sir."

Sir picked it up, turned it on . . .

And put it back down. "Too bad!" he chirped, downright *gleeful*, stepping back in front of Nicky and spinning the cross until Nicky was upside down. "You know, I hear that if you rip the hair from the follicle"—and here he paused to demonstrate by pulling two from Nicky's inner thigh—"it won't grow back for weeks. I wonder"—another hair, and another, this time from his ankle—"how long it will take people to notice that you've got no," *pluck,* "hair below the neck," *pluck,* "at all."

WRAPPED UP

Devon imagined it was like being buried alive. Damp and stifling, eight solid feet of impenetrable fear pressing down until it crushed you.

On TV, the shortstop fumbled the ball, and somebody stole third base. He wasn't even sure which teams were playing. His focus was on his pet. His little Houdini. Mummified. Buried alive.

The poor thing could struggle all he wanted; there was no getting out of this one.

And just to remind him of exactly that, Devon reached down and stuck the pad of his thumb over the little length of tube jutting from Nicky's duct-tape shroud, cutting off his only source of air. He felt suction against his thumb, a futile struggle to suck in oxygen. In a moment, a whole new struggle would begin. That beautiful body, second-skinned with saran wrap and duct tape from head to toe, would buck and heave, expending oxygen it didn't have. And for what? Nicky couldn't even wiggle a finger. He was wrapped too hard, taped too close, palms bound flat against the tops of his thighs (and how miserably uncomfortable that must be by now!), body straight and taut. A pretty pale Tutankhamen wrapped in silver instead of gold.

It had to be a hundred degrees in there. Nicky was no doubt *baking* in all that tape and plastic. He was managing tiny little squirming motions—half an inch here, half an inch there—that were surely costing him most of his air and all of his strength. A desperate, starving whisper of a moan floated up through the tube and bumped against Devon's thumb; Devon lifted his hand and allowed the sound to escape, allowed air to return in exchange. Nicky stilled, his head now simply resting on Devon's lap instead of pushing against it. The moaning ceased.

Foul ball. Strike. Third out. On the screen, the teams switched places. But the real show was next to him on the couch. He'd never done this before. Hadn't realized how enthralling it could be. He waited until Nicky's chest fell and rose, fell and rose—the only hint of motion that bound body could achieve without considerable effort—and on the crest of the next rise, he stuck his thumb over the tube again. For a moment he wished he hadn't taped Nicky's face; he wanted to see it, pink and panicked, creased with triumph and submission and pain, those bright blue eyes opening on a high as he tripped, flew, soared right over and through the ties that bound him.

The inning ended. Nobody scored. He let Nicky breathe for a while.

Thirty-nine minutes. How long was too long? Nicky could safeword through the tube if he'd had enough, Devon had made sure of that. But still . . .

He worried too much, he knew; Nicky rarely had enough. If he hadn't wanted his boundaries pushed, he wouldn't have escaped from the comparatively palace-like puppy cage that Devon had left him in to sleep. How he'd done it, Devon had no idea; he would beat the answer out of Nicky later, or maybe fuck it out of him. Probably both at once. But for now it was a mystery. When he'd come into the dungeon to find his pet loose, Nicky had simply smirked and shrugged, held his tongue even when Devon fished out a roll of plastic wrap and a triple-pack of duct tape. *Get out of* this*, Houdini,* Devon had said. Yet still Nicky stood with that same shit-eating *smile* on his face as Devon wrapped him, slowly and with the utmost attention, neck to toe. The smile finally faltered when Devon pulled a clear plastic bag over Nicky's head, gathering it taut and taping off the neck before bothering to poke a breathing hole.

He'd let Nicky watch the whole thing, right up until the very last strip of tape had gone over his eyes. *Then* Nicky struggled—almost twenty minutes of fighting before he exhausted himself and went still. He hadn't torn loose a single strip of tape the whole time. He hadn't even been able to lift his head from Devon's thigh. But Devon liked it when Nicky squirmed. Another thumb over Nicky's air tube, and Devon got what he wanted.

Forty-seven minutes. Things were starting to feel an awful lot like a test of wills, and Devon hated those, because in the end Nicky always won. The boy could take much more pain than Devon could take risks with Nicky's safety. The only way to win was as it had been since the beginning: leaving him alone, tied and ignored. But Devon couldn't very well leave him alone like this. *When the game ends*, he told himself. He'd free him when the game ends. They were already in the top of the ninth.

But the score was tied.

Devon covered the tube with his entire hand, fingers and thumb digging into Nicky's tape-covered cheeks as Nicky struggled. *God*, it went straight to Devon's cock when Nicky whimpered like that. He took his palm off the tube and used it instead to slap Nicky in the head. A second time, and Nicky grunted. Devon wondered if he'd just yanked him from his free-fly, made him lose his focus. He listened for so much as a whispered hint of a safeword. Heard nothing. Unzipped his pants and grabbed himself.

"You hear that, Nicky?" No response. Devon began to stroke himself, moaning loudly. With his free hand, he slapped Nicky again. "You hear that?" A hum, vaguely affirmative, *very* needy. "Yeah . . . you *wish* that was your hand on my cock now, don't you, Nicky."

Another hum, louder this time. Devon groped roughly at Nicky's crotch. Even through the layers and layers of plastic wrap and tape, he could see a bulge trying to form. Little puffs of air, hot and fast, came out the end of the tube as Nicky tried to press his hips into Devon's hand. He got about a quarter inch off the couch before he exhausted himself and fell back.

Devon jerked off hard and loud. Neither one of them got to breathe through his climax. He shot all over Nicky's tape-covered chest, and when the last of the tremors stopped and his heart rate returned to normal, he plucked the bandage shears off the coffee table and set Nicky free.

The boy looked *wrecked*, panting and flush and soaked in his own sweat. The wrapping was stiff, unpleasantly damp and slippery. Devon cracked Nicky out of it like a lobster from its shell. Nicky lay there—lost, insensate, eyes half closed and mind still flying high—as Devon manhandled him free. He didn't help at all. Probably couldn't if he wanted to.

Devon stroked Nicky's sweaty hair off his forehead, leaned down and kissed him on the corner of the mouth. Nicky tried to kiss back, but seemed to possess neither the energy nor the coordination for a proper effort. Devon chuckled, nipped at Nicky's lower lip. "Come on," he said. "Let's get you cleaned up."

Nicky's head rolled ever-so-slowly toward Devon. "Huh?" he breathed. Devon chuckled again; Nicky wasn't tracking, probably hadn't been for the last twenty minutes.

"I said it's bath time, babe. Come on."

Devon didn't wait for Nicky to sit up—he'd have been here for hours if he had. He just tucked one arm under Nicky's shoulders and the other under Nicky's knees and hefted him against his chest.

Nicky was a wiry little thing, but six feet of lean muscle was still an armful and a half, so their trip to the bathroom was a bit stumbly, a bit rushed. Nicky didn't seem to notice; he just clung to Devon's neck and pressed his sweaty face to Devon's chest, mouthing absently at whatever skin he found there. Still gone, then. Devon smiled as he lowered Nicky into the empty tub. He'd done good for his boy today.

The shock of cold enamel seemed to wake Nicky a little. He gasped, flailed upright with a breathy "Whu—?" but then caught sight of Devon's smiling face and leaned back again, shut his eyes and mumbled, "Thank you, Sir."

Devon kissed him again, this time on the top of the head—no pressure for Nicky to work up the ability to kiss him back, that way— and whispered in Nicky's ear, "You're welcome, love. Anytime."

And damn if he wasn't the luckiest fucking guy in the world to be able to say that.

ONE FOR THE ROAD

Sir is usually home well before I am, but today they've sent me off early to pack and catch a nap before leaving for LA. I've packed, but I've not bothered with sleeping; Sir will be home any minute, and before I lead the charge on a week-long promotional blitz from one end of Hollywood to the other, I want someone to take charge of *me*.

So I wait for him in the foyer by the front door, where he will see me the moment he walks in. Sitting on my heels, legs spread, hands lying limp on my knees. Naked but for collar and cuffs. The marble tiles are cold and hard beneath me. I could wait on the runner, plush and warm, but there are no runners in the space I wish to occupy for the next little while.

The door bangs open some time later and Sir blusters through, hands full and keys dangling from his mouth. He catches sight of me and I detect a moment of surprise, then amusement, then lust, and then a hard shell of irritation and command. He spits his keys at me and says, "Don't just sit there. Help me."

I rise to my feet without using my hands—just how he likes—and take two bags of groceries and his courier bag from his arms. Thus freed, he closes the door and locks it, then follows me to the kitchen. I unpack the groceries in silence, noting the makings of one of Sir's elaborate suppers he loves to cook for me when he finally can't stand to watch me eat TV dinners for the tenth day in a row. My heart sinks—I won't be here long enough to enjoy it. Well, I will simply have to make it up to him, find another way to please him instead.

When I bend to place the lettuce in the crisper, he smacks my upturned ass with a heavy, open palm. I yelp and bang my head on a plastic shelf, but I barely notice over the stinging tingles racing from the back of my pelvis to the front.

"Come here," he says. I oblige and am rewarded with a bruising kiss, both his hands wrapped around my head, his hips grinding me into the refrigerator door. He uses his cheek to mush my nostrils shut, starving me of air as the kiss draws on.

I make a faint little noise as my lungs begin to burn and my cock stiffens against his clothed hip, bang my fists against the fridge as the world starts to gray. At last he lets up, pulls his tongue from my mouth and his face from mine. His body stays pressed to me, supporting me against the door as I gulp air through swollen, tingling lips. His hands stay firm on my head, spinning dizzy with arousal and oxygen.

Sir licks his lips and asks, in that thrilling tone that demands replies of the utmost speed and brevity, "Why are you home so early?"

I'm still panting, but I answer quickly. "First interview got pushed up to seven tomorrow morning."

Sadness flits across his face, then disappointment, then anger. He pushes me harder against the fridge—the chrome doors are shocking cold against my bare back—and says, "I was going to make you dinner."

"I know, Sir. I'm sorry, but I leave in . . ." A quick glance at the clock over the stove before turning my eyes back to Sir's chest. "Eighty-seven minutes." I allow my hands to wander to Sir's hips, barely touching. "Please let me make it up to you."

He steps back and knocks my hands away, then delivers twin stinging slaps to my nipples. "Did I say you could touch me, Nicky?"

I hang my head and mumble, "No, Sir," trying not to let my disappointment show.

"I'll use you when I'm good and ready, understand?"

"Yes, Sir."

He snaps his fingers and says, "Come," then ambles off toward the bedroom. Adds, "Crawl," before I can take a single upright step. I drop happily to my hands and knees and race to catch up with his feet, which I have an overwhelming desire to kiss, to touch, to worship if he'll let me. We enter the bedroom together, and he stops near the bed, spreading his arms and legs.

I take my cue to undress him, beginning with his shoes and socks, placing a loving, lingering kiss on each ankle, instep, and toe as I expose them. I steal a touch by dragging my hands up his thighs before unbuckling his belt; he chuckles and pets me atop the head, but holds his hand out for the belt once I've pulled it through its loops. It's with a mix of trepidation and thrill that I turn it over to him, eager for what might come next.

When nothing does, I attack the button of his pants with my tongue and teeth, unhooking and then unzipping him without using my hands—a promise of my skills, of how I'll worship him if he'll let me. Another chuckle from Sir, another head pat, and then he loops his belt beneath my chin and uses it to tilt my head back until I'm looking into his smiling eyes.

"Well, well, someone's eager today, huh?" The belt disappears from my chin, reappears with a teasing flop against my left shoulder. I nod vigorously—yes to my eagerness, yes to his belt on my skin, yes to everything he has the power to give and take.

The belt connects again, much harder this time, makes a delicious *thwap* against my skin. I close my eyes just long enough to sink into the sensation before returning my gaze to him, as adoring as I know how to make it.

"Will you still be gone five days?" he asks. "Speak."

"Yes, Sir."

He hits me again. Again. Then thrice more: once for each day I'll be taking myself from him. The fifth one leaves me gasping, knocks me onto my hands. My cock bumps my thigh, and I have to curl my fingers into the carpet to stop from touching myself. I roll my shoulders instead, relishing the burn, imagining the welts rising on my skin. Imagining, just for a moment, what people might say if one showed on camera.

"Well then," he says, pushing his unfastened pants down and kicking them behind him. "Looks like you've got five days' worth of cock to suck in the next sixty minutes."

I nearly dive for him, but he steps away, props some pillows up against the headboard and arranges himself on the bed so that he can watch me work. After an achingly protracted settling in, he nods me over. I climb up between his spread legs and set myself fully to the task, gently grasping his balls in one hand and the base of his cock in the other before sucking the head into my mouth. I know exactly how he likes it, slow and rhythmic, a little twist of the hand on each upstroke, a hard suck followed by a swipe of the tongue on each downstroke. He is quiet, as he always is, but his breathing picks up fast and one of his hands tangles tight and painful in my hair.

When at last he loses patience with my pacing—but really, he can't possibly blame me for wishing to prolong this, to make the taste and feel and joy of him last as long as possible—he uses that hand to shove my nose down to his pubic hair. I take the message and am more than happy to deep-throat him on my own, but am happier yet when he decides to guide me, holding my head still and using my mouth at his own speed.

When Sir freezes in place, arched up off the bed with his cock shoved so far down my throat I can't breathe even through my nose, I'm sure he's about to come, awash with the pride of accomplishment and the keen anticipation of his taste on my tongue. But he simply holds there, perfectly still and rock hard, depriving me of oxygen in a frankly remarkable show of self-control. My hands tighten on his thighs and my throat begins to convulse around him, my overstressed gag reflex sending tears down my face.

"Aaaah," he purrs, swiping at a tear with his free hand. "That's what I wanted to see." He wipes away another tear and pops his damp finger into his mouth. The sight of him sucking *anything* like that makes me waste what little air I have left moaning desperately around his cock. I think I mumble "Please," but I'm too far gone to be certain. My head is swimming. I'm seeing spots. And at the rate we're going, I might come all over the comforter before he ever even touches me. Or worse, before he gives me permission.

"Poor little thing," Sir says, voice dripping with sarcasm. "Poor, hungry little thing." He thrusts once in and out of my mouth; I gulp air desperately in the fraction of a second I have before his cock lodges itself back in my throat. "You want so much, don't you."

Another thrust, another gulp of air. I nod as much as his cock and hand will allow me and mumble "Yes Sir!" though it comes out completely unintelligible.

"You want *this*, don't you." Another thrust, hard enough to set me gagging. I nod again, fighting his hand and my shuddering throat to make myself clear—I want it. I want it *so bad*. "Bet you want to breathe, too, don't you."

I eye him over his cock but do not nod; though my hitching chest wants air *right now*, my straining cock and swimming head have other, better ideas.

"Well," Sir drawls, "I can solve both your problems at once. I'm a generous master, after all." The hand tangled in my hair yanks sharply to the left, pulling me off his cock and out from between his legs. I take the hint and roll onto my stomach beside him, heart pounding, body tingling from my toes to my teeth, panting like a dog in the hot sun. He's on me before I've taken three breaths, in me before I've taken four, penetrating hard without warning or prep or any lube but my copious spittle.

I shout with the shock of it, the searing pleasure inseparable from the pain, and work my way up onto my knees to make his thrusting easier. His hand snakes around my hip, and again I'm afraid I'll explode if he touches me, that I'll come far too soon and without permission. But he knows me so well; he pinches two strong fingers around the base of my cock and cuts off any chance of that happening. The touch drives me crazier despite that—pushes me to the bleeding edge without letting me fall over it. I moan out my frustration, my pleasure so sharp I can hear it, smell it, taste it like come in the back of my throat, so enveloping it drowns out everything but him, but Sir, and I'm calling his name over and over as he pounds into me, uses me, owns me completely.

Awash in him as I am, I fail to notice his rising grunts, his quickening pace, until he grits out "Come for me, Nicky!" and removes those two pinching fingers from the base of my cock. He strokes me once, twice, before I shoot over his hand and up my stomach with a cry. His own cry follows a second later as he buries himself deep and stills his hips against my ass, riding out the last of his orgasm, his hands stroking warm and gentle over the welts on my back.

"Good boy," he whispers, leaning over to pepper kisses across my shoulders, down my neck. "My good boy." He disentangles from me and turns me over gently, then lies atop me. "I'll miss you," he says between nibbles and licks. His lips trail down my chin, my neck, stop just below my collarbone and set to work on a patch of skin there. Teeth follow lips, and he bites me so hard I gasp, try to squirm away. He pins my body with his own and doesn't let up with his teeth until I'm whimpering like a child, batting my fists against the bed and squeezing my eyes closed against tears. But he knows me perfectly, stops just before it becomes too much, and soothes the mark with a skilled, gentle tongue.

"To remember me by," he says, lapping once more at the already-bruising bite. "While you're gone."

I cannot help it—I snort out a laugh. As if I could ever forget him.

PONY UP

I 've never liked holiday parties. The crowds, the noise, the strangers, the acquaintances you haven't seen in ten years whose names you're somehow supposed to remember, the open-bar abuse, the terrible music, the stupid games, the mistletoe that everyone thinks it's so funny to maneuver you beneath . . .

I don't like weddings either, pretty much for all the same reasons, nor am I a fan of the wrath-of-nature-tempting elitism that are gated beach communities. Which makes a Christmas wedding in Boca Raton a whole new level of hell, even if it is a total kinkfest—just as much a collaring, really, as a marriage under God.

So what, you may ask, am I doing here?

Well, for starters, I didn't exactly have a choice. At least I can't hear the music, and I'm well away from the drunken crowd and the mistletoe. Fuck, I'm not even in the house. Which is probably for the best, because the only thing I'm wearing is a Santa hat . . . unless you count the big red bow tied around my cock and balls.

I guess that makes me a wedding present. Not sure why Sir stowed me in the barn, then, instead of drafting me into wait-service like the rest of the Santa-hatted slaves I saw on my way past the party, but I guess I shouldn't complain. They're all working their naked little butts off, while I get to lounge in the climate-controlled barn and nap. Which, admittedly, would be easier if my own naked little butt weren't half buried in itchy straw.

On the other hand, I'd rather be serving Sir—even serving Sir's friends—than be sitting here alone. I wonder who's fetching him drinks, bringing him food, licking his fingers clean and following him round the dance floor. I wonder if he's thinking of me as he sips one of those girly drinks he loves so much, dancing and laughing and maybe even taking his turn at reddening the slave-groom's ass when the boy's master puts his prize on display.

I wonder, briefly, what Sir's intent was in gifting me. The happy couple already comprised a slave; wouldn't my presence just make the poor boy jealous? Or was he a switch, interested in playing for a night alongside his master instead of beneath him? That thought excites me more than I care to admit; the red bow around my cock and balls tightens like Sir's talented fingers as my body responds. I reach down to touch myself, just once, then curl my fingers into fists and tuck them back beneath my head before I can break Sir's rules. But it aches, *God,* like a hunger, an unreachable itch. And it won't get better anytime soon; the blood is trapped by the ribbon-cum-cock ring, and my thoughts have turned to dangerous places, to threesomes, to *foursomes*, serving the new couple and Sir all at once, all night long, never allowed to touch myself, never allowed to come . . .

Shit. Enough of that. Truth is, I'm probably just the new dishwasher or something. The thought makes me laugh until I'm breathless. If all they use me for is chores, it would be a sad, sad waste of a gift.

I fall asleep, wake up sometime later stiff and colder than before. The hay prickles and pokes as I stretch, but I don't get up. I kind of like it, for one thing, especially where it scratches against the welts Sir left on my back and ass the night before. Plus, I'm pretty sure I'm not supposed to move, that this is a test, even though Sir said no such thing. Why else would he have left me here unbound, if not to see whether I'd stay put on my own? I've no intention of displeasing or shaming him *or* myself in front of a whole wedding full of Doms and subs.

Which is why I am most definitely not in any way even beginning to contemplate thinking about touching myself without permission, despite my erection having turned nearly the same shade of red as the big velvet bow that's framing it.

It's also why I'm so damn relieved when Sir at last comes to get me that I'm kneeling at his feet and pressing kisses to his dress shoes without even knowing how I got there. He'll rescue me from myself, I know he will.

He always does.

He smiles at me, reaches down to pet my hair, then cups my chin and tugs me to my feet. The kiss he gives me nearly unhinges my knees again, but he's holding on tight.

He always does.

"Good boy," he murmurs against my ear, glancing approvingly at my cock, now weeping hard against his thigh. He says it like maybe he's a little surprised I behaved all this time without the aid of bindings or his watchful eye, and I glow with the knowledge that I've pleased him, impressed him, maybe even exceeded his expectations.

"Stand up straight now," he says. "Arms out."

Someone's boy is at his heel, I realize now, only a little surprised that I'd failed to notice the slave earlier over Sir's commanding presence. Yet he's a lovely thing, truly, perhaps five years my junior, just as fit, a face made just as surely for acting as I've been told my own is so many times. My jealousy takes me by surprise—no one should be at Sir's heel but *me*—and I have to squash it down with clenched fists and jaw when Sir waves him forward and takes two bundles from his outstretched hands.

Said bundles do help a bit, though. One is a rope, the other a jingle of leather and metal. Sir passes the rope back to the boy, who takes it willingly, head down and cock erect. The leather Sir shakes out and fits over my bare shoulders. It's a harness of sorts, wide padded straps crossing over my chest and around my waist and buckling at my back. More straps wend between my legs, a built-in leather cock ring fitting snug beside the velvet bow, a long thin strap of leather dangling down from it and brushing the barn floor. Sir finishes his buckling and reaches into the pocket of his tuxedo jacket, pulls out . . .

A horse tail?

Oh, *fuck*. The barn, the harness . . . How did I not see this coming?

The grin he tosses me when realization dawns across my face is positively evil.

"Ass up, boy," he says through that wicked grin, and I spread my legs wide, bend over, and grab my ankles. Cold lube squirts against my hole—he must have had a little packet in there along with the horse tail—and then a plug that feels the size of Sir's wrist is being worked inside me. I haven't been fucked in three days and I'm way too tight now for something that big to go in easy—assuming a plug that big could *ever* go in easy. It hurts; my fingers make dents at my ankles and my poor neglected cock stands up taller than ever, shouting *Pay attention to me!* to anyone who will listen.

Sadly, no one is. At least not now. Possibly not at all tonight.

Which, of course, just makes my cock stand up taller yet.

"Almost there, Nicky," Sir says, his free hand resting warm and firm in the small of my back to comfort me, or perhaps just to stop me from falling over. But he's true to his word; with one last hot flash of pain the flare pops inside me, and my muscles clench tight around the neck of the plug, drawing it in even deeper. Horsehair tickles at my asscheeks and all the way down to the backs of my knees. I feel so full it's like his whole fucking fist is inside me. *Fuck*, if so much as the breeze blows too strong across my cock, I might well shoot my load, permission or no.

"Stand up now, Nicky," Sir says, the unmistakable pride in his voice flushing me head to toe. My eyes catch the other slave's gaze for a moment as I straighten, and this time, it's *he* who's jealous of me.

Sir reaches for the long thin strap of leather still dangling from the harness cock ring and runs it up my asscrack over the horse tail, then buckles it tight to the harness near my shoulders. My hands are buckled into the harness next, resting comfortably at the small of my back, no strain at all on my shoulders or wrists.

Done binding me, Sir takes the rope from the silent slave behind him—actually two ropes; reins, to be specific—clips them to a ring down near my balls, and runs them out behind me. A sharp tug on one pulls my bound cock and balls to the left with a bright spark of pleasure-pain; a tug on the other pulls my junk to the right. I suppose I won't be needing a bridle, then.

Sir seems satisfied. He gathers up the reins in one hand, cups my elbow in the other, and leads me outside into the cold.

Well, more like into the lukewarm and sticky—your average cloying Florida night. A light breeze blows against my bare skin, raising goosebumps in its wake. Walking is . . . *difficult* with this plug inside me, every step jostling and turning it, rubbing it along my prostate (and possibly the back of my fucking throat), making the horsetail swish and sway. A bug buzzes nearby and, denied my hands, I find myself wishing the tail were real so I could swat the damn thing away. Sir leans in and does it for me.

He guides me around the massive home, clumps of partygoers with drinks in hand watching appreciatively as I pass them by. I duck my eyes like a good boy, but not too soon to miss more jealous looks from naked boys and girls stuck carrying trays of food and drink. Fierce pride gathers low in my belly (or maybe that's just my looming orgasm?); any one of these pets could have been chosen to pull the wedding carriage, but the grooms picked *me*. *Sir* picked me.

In the backyard now, down toward the narrow strip of sandy beach, the ocean churning steadily under endless strings of party lights and a near-full moon. A band plays sappy music while couples sway on the outdoor dance floor. A hundred or so others are sitting at white-draped tables, eating wedding cake and other delicacies from silver carts being wheeled through the tables by pretty naked pets in silly Santa hats. I feel eyes on me and straighten my spine, square my shoulders like Sir taught me and high-step toward the beach. Sir leans in and praises me, breath tickling the shell of my ear with the promise of pleasure, of reward.

My shiver runs straight down to my toes.

Sir marches me past the crowd, down to where the sand is packed hard and damp from the receding tide. There awaits a magnificent carriage, decked all in white satin, room for two and two alone on the padded bench seat above its tall wheels. I move to stand before it without being told, hear the grooms climb inside while Sir hooks my harness to the carriage shaft. It doesn't look any heavier than the bike-drawn carriages tourists take through Manhattan, but added to the weight of the grooms and the drag of wet sand, I suspect I'll soon be getting one of the tougher workouts of my life.

Sir hands someone my reins, and I'm treated to two hard tugs again, first to the right and then the left. I was ready for that, but not for the stripe of fire that lands across my shoulders a second later; I yelp, jump, take half a step forward and feel the weight of the cart drag at the straps around my chest. From somewhere just behind me, Sir chuckles and says, "That's it, Bill. Don't spare the whip; he likes it."

I grin to myself and roll my shoulders as the blaze fades to embers; truer words have never been spoken.

Sir speaks again, but this time it's to me. "Good ponies get apples and sugar cubes," he says. "If you're a *very* good pony, I'll rub you down and stud you when you get back."

Well, *fuck*. This time, my shiver runs right down through the sand.

I don't know where the grooms will have me take them, or how long I'll be gone, or how raw my back and balls and legs will be by the time they're done with me, but I don't care. I don't even care that I'll love every second of it, though of course I will. In the end, none of that really matters—what *really* matters is that I'm Sir's good boy, and he'll be waiting right here for me, counting the moments until my return just as anxiously as I.

ALSO BY RACHEL HAIMOWITZ

ABOUT THE AUTHOR

Rachel is an M/M erotic romance author, a freelance writer and editor, and the Managing Editor of Riptide Publishing. She's also a sadist with a pesky conscience, shamelessly silly, and quite proudly pervish. Fortunately, all those things make writing a lot more fun for her . . . if not so much for her characters.

When she's not writing about hot guys getting it on (or just plain getting it; her characters rarely escape a story unscathed), she loves to read, hike, camp, sing, perform in community theater, and glue captions to cats. She also has a particular fondness for her very needy dog, her even needier cat, and shouting at kids to get off her lawn.

You can find Rachel at her website, http://rachelhaimowitz.com, tweeting as @RachelHaimowitz, and on Goodreads.com.

She loves to hear from folks, so feel free to drop her a line anytime at metarachel@gmail.com.

Enjoy this book?
Find more BDSM at
RiptidePublishing.com!

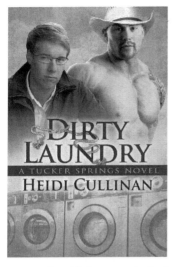

www.riptidepublishing.com/titles/
dirty-laundry

www.riptidepublishing.com/titles/
power-play-resistance

Earn Bonus Bucks!

Earn 1 Bonus Buck for each dollar you spend. Find out how at
RiptidePublishing.com/news/bonus-bucks.

Win Free Ebooks for a Year!

Pre-order coming soon titles directly through our site and you'll
receive one entry into a drawing to win free books for a year! Get the
details at RiptidePublishing.com/contests.

3337504R10065

Printed in Great Britain
by Amazon.co.uk, Ltd.,
Marston Gate.